the
hungry
place

the
hungry
place

jessie
haas

BOYDS MILLS PRESS
AN IMPRINT OF BOYDS MILLS & KANE
New York

For information about permission to reproduce selections from this book,
please contact permissions@bmkbooks.com.

This is a work of fiction. Names, characters, places, and incidents are products of the author's imagination or are used fictitiously. Any resemblance to actual events, locales, or persons, living or dead, is entirely coincidental.

Boyds Mills Press
An imprint of Boyds Mills & Kane, a division of Astra Publishing House
boydsmillspress.com
Printed in the United States of America

ISBN: 978-1-68437-794-7 (hc)
ISBN: 978-1-63592-383-4 (eBook)
Library of Congress Control Number: 2019953785

First edition
10 9 8 7 6 5 4 3 2 1

Design by Anahid Hamparian
The text is set in Minion Pro.
The titles are set in Minion Pro.

To my true love, my sweet pony,
and all who've helped me with this story.
(You know who you are, Rebecca M. Davis!)
Many thanks.

Contents

the
spell

SHE was born in a stall, on a bed of golden straw. Her mother's warm tongue washed and kissed her. Her mother's voice spoke to her in a deep chuckle that she understood perfectly: *love, love, love.*

There was another voice, too, rich like her mother's, also speaking of love, but in a different way. "A filly? Perfect. You know what to do, Charlie." The voice came from a large being standing close by, a being not of their kind, but one who belonged here.

But someone else crouched above her, restraining her, moving her, taking power over her. She looked up into the thin, sharp face of one of that other kind of being and stiffened. She would move when *she* chose, not because some other creature made her.

It was stronger than she was.

"Bend her legs," the voice said. "Gently, gently. When she resists like that, just hold and wait till she gives in."

But she must be free! She surged against the holding with all her might.

It made no difference. Her mother kept bathing her, saying *All is well.*

So all was well? It must be. Her mother said so.

"There!" The deep, kind voice. "She just submitted. They learn like lightning at this age. They have to, in the wild. Anything we can teach them now they never forget. It's like a spell to protect her from fear and confusion. You're the good fairy, Charlie, blessing the princess in her cradle."

"Let's hope there's no wicked stepmother," said a second voice, above her, so close it vibrated through her skin. Not as deep, not as kind. Already she knew which voice she preferred.

Both were blurred by the rumble of her mother saying *Mine. Perfect. Get up!*

It seemed important, so she arranged two legs in front of herself and heaved. Cool air beneath her belly, then *thump!* She was down again. Her mother's tongue rubbed her vigorously. *Get up!*

Up, then. She scrabbled in the loose bedding around her, surging, spreading her four legs wide to stop from swaying.

"Oh *my!*" The kind voice was as joyous as her mother's. "We have something very special here!"

"You can't tell at this age."

"This is the best age to tell, if you have the eye. And I do!"

Meanwhile, her mother, with nickers and nudges, was

asking for more. *More?* She was up. What more was there to do? Her legs wobbled and buckled beneath her. She straightened the bendy parts in the middle and swung one long stem forward. Now the legs were uneven. That didn't feel right. Push another one forward. Another. Another. They trembled. Her mother nickered. *Come here.*

She struggled on, step by step, until she bumped into her mother's warm flank. The scent was sweet and well known, though this was the first time she had smelled it. Her mother's big belly swelled above her. Her mother's neck arched around her. Her mother's warm tongue kissed and also pushed, still pushed, toward a place that smelled even sweeter and woke up a new feeling in her middle and on her tongue.

Hungry!

She reached up, bumping, searching—*oh!* Milk trickled down her throat and into the hungry place, and there was more, and there was more. Her short tail wiggled. The kind voice said, "I never get tired of seeing that. Makes it all worthwhile."

When the hungry place was filled, her legs wanted to fold. She struggled to stay on top as they trembled and buckled and—*whump!* Safe in the bedding, full and warm and quite tired already—life was hard work!—her eyes closed.

~

Two men walked out of the barn side by side, one large and puffing slightly, the other slender and light-footed as a junkyard dog. They passed under the arched sign. Moonlight picked out the letters: *Highover Farm, Champion Connemara Ponies. Roland McDermott, proprietor.* Above them the big house stood tall as a castle, only one downstairs window shining yellow. Below them stretched a pale meadow, edged by dark trees that fell away, ridgetop beyond ridgetop, into the valley.

The larger man paused, looking back at the barn. "You'll get the vet in first thing in the morning, Charlie."

"I always do."

"Don't mind my fussing. I've bred some fine ponies on this hill, but mark my words—that's the one this farm will be remembered for." The old man took a cautious breath, pressing his fist against his chest. "And not a moment too soon!" He walked slowly up the slope to the big house.

The smaller man watched him go. His teeth showed in the moonlight. "Careful, old boy," he murmured. "You're the meal ticket around here." He waited, while the door of the big house opened and closed, and a bulky form passed the window.

Then he turned toward the trainer's cottage. It was a normal-size house, in fact, but the barn and big house made it seem modest. Every window blazed with light. When the trainer walked in, his wife looked up from her embroidery, a dark-haired woman with a hard, handsome face.

"The old mare had a filly," the trainer said. "*He* thinks she's the one he's been waiting for. Looks like just another pony to me—but he's got the eye, he says."

"He does have an eye," the wife said. "For ponies. Lucky for us there's a lot he *doesn't* see."

spine
of steel

"RAE, what do you want for your birthday?" Gammer asked. She spoke from a computer screen on the kitchen table of a small house, across the ridgetops and many miles away from Highover.

Rae leaned close to her face on the screen. She could almost smell fresh lemons. This was the season for lemon pies in Florida. "A pony," she said. "A real pony of my own."

Gammer smiled. "Lovebug, you've hungered for a pony since you were old enough to say the word. You get that from your mama. What I meant was, what do you want that I can give you? I don't get rich making pies, you know. I get *by*."

Rae had heard this before, but tonight it seemed important. "What does getting by *mean*, exactly?"

"It means I have enough," Gammer said. "I can keep myself fed, keep the lights on, live the life I picked out for myself, with a little surplus for emergencies. But not a pony-size surplus. Besides, taking on an animal is a big decision. Your daddy would need to agree."

"But you asked what I wanted," Rae said.

"That I did, lovebug!"

"Are *we* getting by? I mean, is Daddy?"

"Oh yes! Your daddy's a smart man. He doesn't need as much cash-money as other people do. Driving the garbage truck lets him be home when you get back from school, and gives him time for his sculptures. He's doing what he loves, and yes, he's getting by. He gives you a good life, doesn't he?"

"It would be a good life if I had a pony." Rae didn't say this very loudly.

The computer barked. Gammer reached down out of view and picked up a small scruffy dog. "Look, Monkey, there's Rae! Say hi to him, Rae."

"Hi, Monkey!"

Monkey barked again. Outside on the porch Rae's big dog, Thor, barked in response and scratched at the door to be let in.

"Look at the commotion you've caused!" Gammer told Monkey. "Hush now! We'll be home in a couple of days. You can play with your friends then."

Rae's father came into the room. "Better wind things down," he said. "It's getting late."

"We're talking about my pony," Rae said. "The one I'm going to have someday."

"Are you? Well, five more minutes then." He went out of the room. Gammer leaned forward so her face filled the computer screen. Monkey leaned in too, licking her cheek.

"Stop it, Monkey! Lovebug, we'll talk more about this when I get home. It's too important for a five-minute conversation. You wait for me, and please don't bother your daddy about it."

"I wasn't going to *bother* him," Rae said. "I was just going to ask."

Gammer said, "And I'm asking you to wait. Now tell me, what *do* you want that I might be able to get for you? A model pony? You love your models."

Rae understood what she'd just been told. Don't ask. Not for *that*. Not now. Still, she was getting older—not too old for models, but she wanted something more serious. Something real. "A book," she said finally. "One that tells how to take care of a pony."

Gammer leaned back from the computer. "You have a spine of steel, lovebug! Well, I imagine I might be able to find something like that. Say good night, Monkey!"

Monkey barked. Thor rushed into the room, barking too, and reached up to lick the computer screen. "Yuck!" Rae said, laughing.

Later in her room, though, she didn't feel like laughing. Rae didn't sprinkle ponies on her lunchbox or her underwear. She had them here on her walls, real looking in posters and photos, real seeming in books on her shelf. Her walls were the color of a stall, and her curtains were the color of grass. Up here, she sometimes felt that she actually did have a pony, or perhaps several. Not tonight.

She looked out her bedroom window. The moon shone on the barn's rusty roof and the grass beside it, the grass that Rae's pony would someday eat. That barn and grass for the someday

7

pony were the whole reason her parents had bought this house, so she'd always been told. She would have a pony now, if Mom hadn't died.

Rae barely remembered Mom. She had Mom's horse books, some riding pants that didn't fit yet, a belt with a buckle that Dad made out of a real hoof pick—and a hunger in her heart, the same one Mom had had. It couldn't be explained. "Why do you love ponies? Why do you love horses?" The true answer never satisfied anyone. I *just do*. It was too simple. Rae only knew one other person who understood, and they weren't friends anymore.

A spine of steel. Did she really have that?

She hoped so. She felt like she was going to need one.

chapter 3

a princess

SHE blinked her eyes open in a golden sunbeam—another new thing.

Hungry!

Her mother stood nearby, crunching something. She turned her head and invited. *Come.*

She'd gotten up and eaten five times overnight, and each time had been easier. Now she organized her legs, told them firmly what to do, and in a moment she was up, braced and ready, and in another moment she was having another meal. *So good!*

The half door opened, letting in the large round shape of the old man. He had two legs, not four, but otherwise looked not so different from her mother. A warm hand rested on her back. She wasn't afraid. Hands were among her earliest memories, and this hand loved her as much as her mother did. Her tail wiggled. Her mother nickered and the old man made a sound that was like a nicker and meant the same thing.

As she finished her meal, someone else came in, on a cloud of pungent smells. "So you got one more foal out of the old lady, Roland," he said.

"Best foal of my life!" the old man answered. He gently guided her forward.

The newcomer stared and nodded. "You may be right."

The man, Roland, swelled even larger than normal. "I'm absolutely right! I have the eye. Look at that slope of shoulder! And the neck. Long and refined—but she's sturdy, too. Look at the depth. Look at the legs!"

"Structurally perfect," the newcomer said. "But there's more. I don't know how to say it—"

"An aura of quality. Her mother gave her that. The charisma, that electric shock when you look at her—that comes from her father."

The newcomer said, "Of course she may outgrow it."

"No. What you can see now, they never outgrow, in my experience—and I have a lot of experience."

"She'll turn gray, of course, like her mother," said the newcomer. "A pity. I do like a black pony."

"I prefer the grays. Though the best color for toughness is dun."

"This one won't need to be tough, not with the life you'll give her," the newcomer said. "All right, let's get to work."

Another person came in. She remembered him also, from the night before—the one who had controlled her. He held her still again, as one more set of gentle hands rubbed her all over, pressed things against her, slid something sharp and slim and cold into her neck, and paused, and slid it out again. That almost hurt—but it almost didn't and her mother stayed calm, so she did too.

The newcomer capped the vial of blood and put it in his pocket. "Congratulations, Roland. A happy day for you."

"A happy day indeed."

He remained behind when the others left. "Congratulations, old lady," he said to the mare. "You've done us all proud. Now your little girl needs a name. Hmmm . . ." The voice paused, and when it came again, it was pointed at the filly. Busy as she was, nosing, tasting, sniffing her way along the walls of the stall, she could hear that.

"Your mama is a queen, and you're her youngest. The youngest princess is always the most beautiful, the kind one, the wise one. Well, why not? *Banphrionsa.*" It sounded like BON-frince-a. "The Irish word for *princess. Highover Banphrionsa.* But that's only for registration papers and show rings. Here we'll call you Princess."

"Princess?" said the trainer's wife, behind him. "That sounds about right!"

"What do you mean?" Roland asked, with an edge to his voice.

The wife was quick to hear it. She smiled at him, making her eyes seem warm and mischievous. It was a trick she had. "Lovely! She's lovely! That's what a princess is—pretty and pampered."

"A make-believe princess, maybe! A *real* princess could become queen at any moment. She needs to be brave and wise,

11

so she can protect her people. That's how I see it, anyhow. But maybe you think I'm an old fool?"

The wife twinkled her eyes at him. "Oh no! But I grew up poor, you know. I've had to work for everything I got. So I never really understood the whole princess thing."

"I see." Roland's voice softened, exactly as she had intended. She grinned a bad girl grin at him.

"I see myself more as the wicked stepmother type," she said. "Or the bad fairy who *doesn't* get asked to the christening and comes anyway."

The trainer, returning just then, caught his wife's eye and made a zipping motion along his lips. She shook her head as if to say, *Don't worry! I know what I'm doing*, and opened the stall door, uninvited. Roland made a gesture to stop her. He got a *Don't worry* head shake as well, as she came toward Princess.

Princess was learning fast, and she was born knowing some old things, deep down. What she heard in the woman's voice made her move closer to her mother.

"No, no, little one! You need my blessing too." Hands closed around her chest. That was familiar enough, but these hands had long painted nails, and when Princess kept moving, they pressed into her.

Truthfully it wasn't the woman digging, it was Princess pushing against her hands. Had she softened her grip even for a moment, Princess would have softened too. Instead the nails pressed harder, and Princess recoiled, throwing up her head. She struck something, hard.

"*Aaagh!*" The hands released. Princess whisked behind the old mare, who swung her body around protectively between her foal and the people. The woman stood pressing both hands to her mouth.

"Are you all right?" her husband asked. "Let me see." He gently pulled her hands away, and she gasped, staring at her palms.

"*Blood!*"

He looked closely at her mouth. "Just a split lip. She bumped you with her head."

"*Just* a split lip!"

"That was unfortunate, Darlene," Roland said, his voice heavy with disapproval. "You've taught her exactly the wrong thing. Now she knows her own strength, and she succeeded in getting away from you. I thought you had more experience than that."

The trainer said, "I'm the one who's worked most with foals. It was an honest mistake."

"I don't want *any* mistakes with Princess," Roland said. "*Ever.*" He approached the mare as he spoke, leaning his crossed arms on her back and looking over at Princess, on the other side. "Hello, little girl. You know me. None of us means you any harm."

It was a reassuring sound, like the sound her mother made, rhythmically chewing hay. Princess took a step closer and raised her nose to sniff his hands. He smelled familiar and pleasant. She tasted a finger.

"That's right, sample everything. It's the way to learn. I wish that hadn't happened," he said over his shoulder. "She'll need careful handling after this, Charlie. Never let her challenge you, never let her suspect that she's stronger than you. You've a light hand with the youngsters—are you up to that challenge?"

No one answered. He turned to find that the couple had already left the stall.

Out in the aisle he found Darlene perched on a director's chair, pressing a tissue to her lip. It was blotched with bright red blood. "Do you need to go for stitches?" Roland asked.

The trainer answered. "It's not that serious."

"Ice it," Roland said. "That always helps. I know you'll forgive me for thinking first of the foal, Darlene."

"Mmm," she said. It could have meant anything.

chapter 4

fences

PRINCESS knew her world completely after a few hours. The bucket. The water in the bucket. The pink salt block. The grain dish. She knew straw. She knew hay and had chewed a strand of it and had watched her mother chew many more. She knew every board along the walls.

But later that day the world changed. The trainer came in the door—Princess knew the door—and opened a second door, completely new to her, on the other side of the stall. Light flooded in, more light than she had ever seen, light so bright it almost hurt. She blinked and stared, but her mother walked straight into it, disappearing in the hazy brilliance. She nickered. *Come.*

Was it safe? It must be. Her mother was out there. Princess gathered herself and jumped high over the line dividing dark from light, into a whole new world.

Air as warm as her mother's breath. A breeze, swirling and tickling over her whole body, laden with new scents and sounds. Leafy trees rustling. Creatures in the air, swooping and chittering. And the rich, familiar voice: "Did you see that, Charlie? A jump worthy of a champion!"

Her mother was eating something on the ground, taking fast bites that made a ripping sound. With every bite, a sweet aroma came up. It made Princess hungry. She put her head down, stretched her neck and her upper lip. But she couldn't even get close. Her legs were too long, or her neck was too short, or both. Finally, she spread her front legs wide. Then her neck was long enough and her nose found—

What was it? A fringe of something, tough and tickly. It was stuck to the ground. When she finally managed to tear off a few blades, they had no taste. She chewed with her baby teeth, and eventually released a flavor, sweet like the smell, but not as strong. Now she was *really* hungry. Time for a snack.

With milk on her whiskers, she felt braver. She wandered away from her mother, gazing, listening, breathing in the new world.

Suddenly her mother called, commandingly. Princess started and turned. She was many yards from the old mare, farther than she'd ever been.

Her legs jumped into action. She streaked across the grass. Amazing! *This* was what legs were for! They knew exactly what to do. Carry her in speedy loops around her mother. Fling up behind her, kicking at the sky. This was *it*!

Soon she was puffing. Her legs felt wobbly and weary. But how did you stop? Princess ran slower, slower, until finally she veered and crashed into her mother. The old mare chortled. Her breath smelled sweetly of what she'd been eating. Princess leaned there, resting, until something moving in the distance caught her eye. She flung her head up, watching the small shapes. They were far away, but her eyes were made for far-seeing. She could see them perfectly, and she knew what they were.

Foals! Like her! They chased one another, sweeping across the field in a large group. They reared and sparred with their long legs, nipped and kicked one another. Princess could feel it in her own legs, which knew how to do exactly what those foals were doing. That field, that herd—that was where she belonged.

I'm coming! She galloped toward them, while behind her a voice cried out, "Charlie! Stop her!" and another yelled, "Whoa!"

White blurs in front of her loomed larger, larger—SMACK! Something threw her flat on her side. A white board fence stood tall over her. Princess scrambled to her feet and galloped along it. Through the spaces between the boards she could see the other foals, paying no attention.

Now there was more fence in front of her. She swerved, twisting her head to look back—but wait, another corner, and now she was running toward her mother, toward the old man and the trainer, toward the open stall door.

She swerved again—and one more time all the way around the paddock. Then, finally, she understood. The fence surrounded her. High and strong, with no gaps, it kept her here, far from the other foals.

Princess stopped. Her sides heaved. She barely had enough breath to send a neigh shrilling across the field.

Here! her mother answered. *Come here!*

Princess tottered toward the old mare. So tired. Her legs collapsed her onto the warm, fragrant grass. After a moment she heard footsteps and voices. The familiar hands of the trainer slid along her legs, pressed against her chest. "She's fine," he said. "Not even a scratch."

"Thank goodness!" Roland's voice sounded weak. "Give me your arm, Charlie. I'd better go sit down."

They went away. Princess took a long, sun-soaked nap while her mother dozed nearby, gently swishing her tail.

When she awakened, and after another meal, Princess walked to the fence and stared at the other foals. She couldn't get there. Fences were solid, even though they didn't look it, and they stopped you.

~

She and her mother were brought back inside. The world went dark, then brightened, and they went out again, and she came to understand the round of a day. The next day the trainer put a set of straps on her head and wrapped a lead rope around her rump. With these he made her move around the stall according to his will. Princess suspected she didn't have to do what he told her. She was strong, wasn't she?

But Roland stood at her mother's head, watching every step. "Careful," he would warn, just as Princess started to wonder if she really had to follow the guidance of the rope and straps. The trainer would release the pressure briefly, then renew it, and she would end up doing what he wanted.

A week passed; days in the bright paddock, nights in the stall, the halter and rope every day, the other foals in the distance.

"Shall I put them out with the others tomorrow?" the trainer asked one afternoon, as he and the old man brought Princess and her mother back to the stall.

"No," Roland said quickly.

"Why not? It's how we raise them."

"True. It's the healthiest way. But we'll be showing her in a few weeks. I don't want any scuffs and scratches."

"We'll be showing her all summer," the trainer said. "Right?"

"That's right," the old man said and turned to go.

The trainer remained, looking over the half door. His wife joined him. "I'm almost sorry for the little thing," the trainer said. "She's too precious to him. He'll never let her be a real pony."

"Princesses never are real." Her voice was hard. "My father used to call me his princess. It didn't stop him from leaving." She laughed, shortly. "Imagine! I used to think my name was *Darling*. I thought I was the best-loved little girl in the world."

The trainer watched her profile, which looked sad and quite beautiful. "I'm sorry," he said. "That happens to a lot of people."

"A lot of people aren't *me*!"

He reached for her hand, and she allowed him to take it. "I'm not an honest man," he said. "I know that about myself. But I have a soft heart. I want to give you everything your father never did."

"That's sweet, Charlie, but I'll look out for myself, too. That's a little more sure."

19

cherries and pits

"RAE, she's here!" Dad called, as Gammer pulled her camper-trailer into the driveway. "My apartment," she called it. She and the apartment spent winters in Florida, where Gammer cooked at a resort. Each spring she drove it home to Rae's front yard where she lived in the warmer months, making pies morning, noon, and night. Gammer's pies were legendary. People planned their vacations around strawberry-rhubarb in June, raspberry in July, blueberry in August, apple and pumpkin in September, October, and November.

Gammer backed the camper into its slot between the blueberry bushes and the vegetable garden. She let Monkey out, and he chased Thor all around the yard. Thor bulged his eyes and let his tongue fly, pretending to be terrified. That was how they celebrated being together again.

Dad, Rae, and Gammer celebrated with hugs and kisses,

with garden-fresh tomatoes and cucumbers from down South, where it was summer already, and mugs of tea. They walked around, looking at Dad's vegetable garden, the chickens, and his new sculptures, all made of pieces of old machinery he picked up on his garbage rounds.

Then Gammer had him lug a bushel box of sour cherries into the kitchen. "I couldn't resist these," she said, "but they need to be made into pie filling right away, before they spoil. Rae, do you want to help? I'm sure your daddy has things he needs to dig or weld."

He did. Gammer and Rae sat at the table with bowls and little plungers that pushed the pits out of the cherries. "I've been missing those quick fingers of yours," Gammer said. "I wouldn't have bought a whole bushel if I wasn't going to have your help."

Their fingers turned red. The bowls in their laps started to fill. Rae waited for Gammer to start the conversation, but Gammer was unusually quiet, unusually serious.

Finally, Rae said, "Should we talk about the pony?"

"Oh, lovebug, I don't want to!" Gammer said. "But you're right, we should." *Sploot!* went the cherry pits out of the cherries and *splink!* into the bowls. After a while Gammer said, "All the way home I've been thinking how to say this. It's not easy, and I'm not even sure it's right. But here goes."

Rae felt her pulse gallop. She looked down at the bowl in her lap.

"I want you to dream big, Rae," Gammer said. "And a pony, for you, is a big, big dream. Almost more than a dream. You were born with that printed on your heart, and it's never going to go away. You're just like your mama that way."

Gammer's busy hands went still in the cherry bowl. "Your grandpa and I could no more afford horses for her than we could afford emeralds, but she found a way to be near them. Any horse—the ugly ones, the wild ones. She loved them more than anything else, till the day she met your daddy—" Gammer wiped tears off her cheeks with the back of one red-stained hand. "Come here, lovebug."

Rae leaned against her, in one of those long, deep hugs she'd been missing all winter. The ache inside her was all mixed up with that missing—missing Gammer, missing Mom, whom she barely remembered, missing the pony she had never had.

"Rae, you need to know this," Gammer said, with her cheek against Rae's hair. "Your daddy may look like a grown-up who knows exactly what he's doing, but he's a young person, too, searching out the way to live *his* dreams and yours. With his garbage run and the food he grows on this little patch of land, he can feed you and take care of you. But he doesn't have the means to feed another animal."

"Ponies don't eat much," Rae said. Her voice was muffled in Gammer's shirt.

"I know," Gammer said. "And your daddy knows how much it means to you. He just doesn't see how to make it happen yet. But we're thinking about it, almost as much as you are. So not too much pressure, sugar-bun. I know you're strong enough to make him miserable. And I know you're strong enough not to."

So not this birthday, Rae thought. That made sense. Dad had been doing nothing to get ready for a pony. She'd been trying to hope that it was his way of making it a bigger surprise, but she couldn't quite make herself believe that.

She straightened up out of the hug and went back to pitting cherries. "I'm getting older, you know."

"Every day older is a day closer to having that pony," Gammer said. "One more day for us to work and save our money. One more day to learn."

"I mean, I'm getting *bigger*. What if I get too big for a pony?"

"Aren't some ponies big enough for adults to ride? I know there was one in the Olympics once."

Big enough for *adults* to ride? She would have to wait till she was an *adult*? A lump formed in Rae's throat, hard and round as a cherry pit. Her hands slowed down.

Gammer reached over and wrapped her own sticky hands around Rae's. "Rae, it *will* happen. I don't know how, and I don't know when, but one day we'll be looking out this kitchen window at your pony. I do believe that!"

"So—I shouldn't ask?"

"*Always* ask!" Gammer said. "I never want you to feel that you can't ask for what you want. But sometimes the answer has to be 'not yet.' And sometimes what you want isn't anything someone else can give you. Sometimes you need to get it for yourself."

Rae was about to turn eight. There were plenty of things she could get for herself. A pony wasn't one of them.

Gammer gave her hands a squeeze and went back to pitting cherries. "Meanwhile, we'll do field trips this summer. Not just to make you feel better, Rae. They'll be educational. You *will* have a pony one day. You'll need to be ready."

Sploot! Splink! went the cherry pits. The one in Rae's throat softened a little. "Where will we go?"

"There's a big show in a few weeks, for one," Gammer said. "I've written it down on my calendar. Then we'll go to farms and riding stables, and—I don't know what all. Your daddy agrees with me. We're not going to pretend this is something you'll outgrow. We're going to support you in every way we can. Does that help, lovebug?"

Rae nodded. She knew it was supposed to help, and maybe it would after a while. Right now? No.

But Gammer was looking anxious. Rae couldn't manage a smile. Instead she *splinked* a cherry pit at Gammer, who *splinked* one back. Monkey, even from the next room, somehow knew that they were playing, and rushed in to bark at them. Gammer was only supposed to play with *him*. So they ended up laughing after all.

But afterward Rae went up to her room. She didn't let herself cry. She needed to feel strong right now, the way Gammer said she was. But the ache came back to her throat when she saw her favorite poster pony—a Shetland, short-legged and almost perfectly round, with a thick mane and heavy winter coat. Every time Rae looked at him, she wanted to bury her fingers deep in his fur.

Already she was almost too tall for a Shetland.

She went to the window. Usually if she blurred her eyes, she could paint whichever pony she chose out there beside the old barn, as vividly as if he was really there. He'd lift his head and prick his ears, almost as though he saw her at the window.

This afternoon it didn't work. The space beside the barn remained empty.

Really, would he ever be there? Because imagining wasn't

enough. Rae wanted to feed him and listen to him crunch his hay. She wanted to kiss the velvety place beside his mouth. She wanted to know him and have him know her—and ride him, yes, but riding was only part of it.

Mom had felt this way. Mom would have made it happen. But all Rae had of Mom were the horse books, her old riding pants (way too big for Rae), and the hoof-pick belt buckle.

She went back downstairs. Gammer stood at the stove, stirring sugar into the cherries. "Your pay is on the table," she said, not turning around.

Pay? Rae picked the money up. Three dollars. "But—"

"I'll make money with these cherries," Gammer said. "You helped, so you should have some of it. Now, do you want to put it in a piggy bank, or a real bank?"

"A real bank," Rae said.

"Then I'll take you tomorrow, and we'll start an account."

chapter 6

a mind of
her own

PRINCESS had seen only the stall, the paddock, and the larger paddock where the other foals played. Was there anything else?

"We need to show her a bit more of the world, to get her ready," Roland decreed, and one day Princess and her mother were led out the front door of the stall, the people door.

They emerged in a broad aisle lined with stalls. Ponies looked over the half doors, pricking their ears in friendly greeting. Princess wanted to go meet them, but she had a halter on her head, and the trainer had her rope in his hand. He didn't pull, but he didn't budge when she strained toward the nearest pony.

So she followed her mother, out of the barn to a gravel driveway lined with trees and some huge gray things, larger than she was and perfectly unmoving.

Princess started toward them. The trainer didn't, and the rope went hard and tight. "Good girl," he said.

Roland often said that. His voice was like her mother's, doting and besotted. When the trainer said it, it was just a sound. He was like that. The things he said sounded wrong. He even said "Princess" like he didn't mean it. Now he was stopping her from doing what she wanted, again. She stood looking at the gray things, one ear tipped back at him. Roland laughed. "She's of two minds about you, Charlie!"

"They don't like to be thwarted," the trainer said.

"Let me take her."

"Are you sure? She isn't trained to lead yet."

"I'll let her lead me. Keep the mare close."

Roland took the rope, and it went soft. The halter stopped pressing Princess's face. She stepped toward the first gray thing and he stepped with her. Together they approached the—what was it?

"That's a rock," he said. "The world is full of them. Great big hard things that you have to go around. And that's another one. Do you want to go see?"

There were six of them, set in a circle under a spreading birch tree. Princess sniffed her way around them. Roland slowly paced beside her, the rope loose between them. "That's right, look them over," he said. "You haven't seen much of the world—"

On the last rock, a small gray hump arched up on four legs, opened a red mouth, and hissed.

Princess jumped back, and Roland stumbled. The rope tightened between the two of them. The trainer's voice barked in the the background: "Careful! Whoa! Are you all right?"

Roland caught his balance and spoke her name. "Princess."

He was breathing fast, but his voice was warm and gentle. Princess looked toward him. The rope softened, and he said, "Good girl! It's just a cat. They're scary when they do that, aren't they?"

His voice drew Princess nearer. He shortened the rope, but it stayed soft. He reached out to rub her neck. "That's my good girl."

Princess peeked past his large stomach at the cat. It sat on the rock, tail wrapped around its paws, looking at her with bright eyes. Though small, it looked dangerous. She was impressed when Roland stretched his hand out to it. "Hello. Where did you come from? We're a long way from civilization up here— and you look like you've seen hard times."

"Must be a stray," the trainer said. "I'll chase it off."

"No, no," Roland said. "He's come this far—he must be meant to be here. Put out a bowl of milk, and get some cat food next time you're in town. He's down on his luck right now, but he looks like he could deal with the mice in the grain room."

"Darlene doesn't like cats," the trainer mentioned.

"It's a big place. I'm sure they can stay out of each other's way."

That night as Princess lay flat on her side near her mother, she was awakened by a new sound—*prrt!* She rolled up on her chest as the cat appeared at the top of the stall door. Princess's mother lifted her head, but didn't get up. Too much trouble.

Princess stood and shuddered the straw off her coat. She stepped toward the cat, ears pricked, legs tight, waiting for a hiss. The cat stiffened, also waiting.

Princess lifted her muzzle. Her warm breath ruffled the cat's fur.

He lashed his tail. But almost in the same moment he arched his back, differently than the first time, and stroked his side against Princess's muzzle. Then he jumped down outside the stall. Princess couldn't see him anymore. She listened to the soft *thumpa-thumpa-thump* of his feet going down the aisle.

The cat came the next night too, and frequently after that. Only for a few minutes. He had many errands, especially after dark. Princess would hear squeaks out in the aisle, then a ghastly crunching. Later the cat might appear for a moment with blood on his breath. They were too different, perhaps, to be close friends, but he was the friend Princess had.

~

After that Princess and her mother were led out every day. The trainer took Princess, and his wife took her mother. He had become bossy, Princess noticed. When she wanted to go in one direction, he was apt to stop her. When she wanted to stand, he'd make her move. He was never simple, always thinking; Princess could feel it, and it made her wary. He was careful and so was she, and she did trust him to a point. But between the thinking and the scent of the woman that persistently clung to him, she was never completely at her ease.

Once they walked down the driveway, along the edge of the big field. Between the rails of the high fence, Princess could see the foals exploring, nibbling grass, scratching each other's shoulders with their teeth. Her shoulders itched just watching them. That place was impossible to reach. She whinnied.

All the ponies raised their heads, pricking their sharp ears.

Then they galloped toward the fence, hooves thundering, manes tossing. The foals cut back and forth between their mothers, nipping, kicking, squealing. They stopped just short of the fence in a cloud of dust and flying clods of turf.

The foals arched their necks at Princess. *Who are you?* The mares made vicious faces at one another and polite ones at Princess's mother. Many were her daughters and grand-daughters. The old mare ignored them, fixing her queenly gaze on the mountains beyond.

"Conceited thing!" said the woman, who was leading her.

A cheeky black colt reached his nose between the rails toward Princess. *Play*, he suggested.

Princess had only ever played by herself, running in circles around her mother. How did you play with another foal? She didn't know—yet she did. All on its own, her mouth took a tiny sideways nip at the black foal's neck.

"Uh-uh-uh!" The trainer pulled her away. "If he puts a mark on your perfect face, what'll happen to me?" He led her up and down the fence, near the other ponies, but out of reach. "Well, she isn't afraid of them. That's what he wanted us to find out. Let's go back to the barn."

He turned Princess after her sedate mother. Princess had always followed her mother before this, always followed the pressure of the rope. Now a wild, stubborn heat flared inside her. *No! Stay!* Her four hooves planted squarely, she twisted her head to look back at the foals.

Gently the trainer tugged on the rope. He could make her move. People were strong. She'd learned that when she was born.

But she was strong too, and she didn't want to go back to the barn.

"Keep going, Darlene," the trainer said. He waited, with a steady pressure on the rope. Princess braced against it, while her mother got farther and farther away. In the distance the old man was calling questions.

"C'mon, Princess," the trainer muttered. "I'm your fairy godmother, remember?"

The other foals got bored and moved away from the fence. Princess was all alone out here with the trainer. Suddenly she wanted her mother. Up flew her head, up flew her short tail, and she came along the driveway at a springy trot, the trainer running beside her. She didn't like that and neither did her mother, who turned, flattening her ears. But they were together again, and after a short meal Princess was ready to follow everyone else back to the barn.

"That didn't go perfectly, Charlie," Roland said, when they got there.

"No. She has a mind of her own," the trainer said. "In spite of the work we did when she was born."

As he led Princess into the stall, he muttered, "Thanks for making me look bad!" He slipped the halter off and Princess moved away from him, toward her mother. But the woman was there, at the old mare's head. Princess hesitated. People were in control. That was the first thing she'd ever learned. But if she didn't go near them? What could they do if she didn't go near them?

At the very least, she would not go near the woman.

She was of a mind to avoid the trainer too, but he always

seemed to know what he would do next, and after all, he was perfectly gentle. Besides, he took her exploring.

~

One day they went inside the horse trailer. Princess's mother ate hay while Princess sniffed things. Doors were closed, an engine started nearby, and Princess felt a vibration beneath her feet. When it stopped and the doors opened, Princess and her mother were led out to a slightly different place in the yard. "Congratulations! Your first trailer ride," the old man said. This happened on several days, until Princess was quite used to it.

The vet came back to give her and her mother more shots. When he was done, he glanced around. "The place looks good, Roland. So the new couple are working out?"

"Yes. Charlie and Darlene are very efficient."

"Where did you say they're from? I thought I knew most of the pony people in this area."

Roland shrugged. "I met them at a show."

"But when you checked their references—"

"I didn't go into all that. I have an eye for people."

"You have an eye for *ponies*, Roland! I've known you to be wrong about people."

"I trust Charlie and Darlene completely! And I trust *you*. About ponies!"

The vet shrugged. "There's no fool like an old fool, Roland. I wish you every success."

After that the daily walks were different. The trainer fussed, wanting Princess to walk slowly, to pose with her front hooves perfectly aligned. Her back hooves had to be lined up too, and her neck stretched high, and her ears pricked forward.

It was hard to hold still. But when she did, Roland said, "*That's* my Princess!" Princess liked knowing she had pleased him. She made herself walk sedately. She stretched her neck and posed for as long as she could.

"She's better for you than she is for me," the trainer mentioned.

"I know." That pleased Roland most of all.

Early one morning Princess and her mother went into the trailer. It moved for a long time, and when it stopped, they were someplace new.

chapter 7

a million dollars

RAE woke in darkness, the morning of the horse show, to the smell of blueberry pie flowing up the stairs. She went down in her pajamas. The kitchen was full of pies—cooling on racks, hissing and bubbling in the oven, raw and white on the table waiting their turn, while Gammer rolled out more dough.

"Good morning, sugar-lamb!"

Rae rubbed her eyes. "Why are you baking? What about the show?"

"I don't want my customers learning to like someone else's pies," Gammer said. "We'll deliver these on our way. If you want to help, you could mix the sugar into the berries."

Rae read the recipe. Carefully she counted out ten cups of sugar and stirred them into the big bowl of berries. She had picked about half those berries. She could do that just as well as Gammer, or maybe even better. When they picked together, it left more time for fun, and put a few dollars in Rae's new bank account.

She measured and mixed in the flour. Gammer added her special dash of spices and poured the berries into the pie shells. "You dot them with butter while I roll out the tops."

Rae sliced off knobs of butter. *Slap slap*, Gammer's rolling pin crisscrossed the dough, laying it out into perfect circles. "This should be interesting," she said. "More ponies than either of us have ever seen in one place. Are you excited, lovebug?"

More ponies than she'd ever seen in one place. Rae was already seeing them in her mind. Staring into space, she added pat after pat of butter, all to one pie.

"Oops!" Gammer redistributed the pats, put the tops on, crimped the edges, and trimmed off the extra dough. Finished pies came out of the oven, raw pies went in. Gammer bundled the crust scraps into a ball, rolled them out in a rectangle, brushed the rectangle with butter, sprinkled it with cinnamon sugar, and rolled it into a tight stick. "Slice these, please, Rae, while I clean up."

Rae took a sharp knife and started slicing the roll of dough into fat sections, spiraled like snails. "Gammer?" she asked. "Do you think I really *will* have a pony someday?"

Gammer swept the snails onto a baking sheet and popped them into the oven. "I never ask myself that kind of question," she said. "What I ask is, *How?*"

"How?"

"How will I do what I want, absent a winning lottery ticket

or a fairy godmother. Years ago I decided to live someplace warm in the winter, and be here with you the rest of the time. I couldn't afford two houses, but if I sold the house I had, I could buy a nice camper. I didn't know how to drive it, mind you, but I learned, and I already knew how to bake pies like few people on earth. It's not a life that would suit everyone, but it's tailor-made for me. *By* me. So don't ask '*Will* I ever,' my love. Ask 'How?'"

"Well. *How?*" Rae asked.

"That's not for me to answer," Gammer said, wiping down the table. "Focus your mind on it. I don't see you as someone who *doesn't* have a pony. You're someone who's *going* to have a pony. A person like that goes to a horse show in a different frame of mind and with her eyes wide open for opportunities."

She poured a cup of coffee and sat down, propping her feet up on a chair. "There! A day's work done before sunup. As soon as those pies are out of the oven, we'll be off."

After a breakfast of scrambled eggs and warm cinnamon snails, they packed the truck with pie boxes.

Rae helped carry the pies into the stores and farm stands. At the last store they bought snacks—organic cherries, cheese sticks, bottles of iced tea, and a fat candy bar each. "Don't tell your daddy," Gammer said. "How often do we do this?"

Now they were really off, the sun rising over the hills, the day starting to get warm. The view out the window got less familiar. Rae watched for ponies in the fields and wondered. What did opportunities look like? Was it possible that today she might see the pony that would one day be hers? Or did opportunity mean something else?

"Oh, here we are," Gammer said, pointing to a sign. *12th Annual Pleasant Valley Animal Shelter Benefit Horse Show.*

She found a parking space, and they started walking through a forest of horse trailers and pickup trucks. Rae pointed at the ground. "Pony poop!"

"Adorable!" Gammer said. They were both laughing as they rounded the final trailer. At last they could see the showground, teeming with people and dogs, golf carts carrying still more people and dogs, and everywhere, horses and ponies.

~

PRINCESS didn't know what most of these things were. People, yes, but there were more different shapes and sizes of people than she had ever seen. And there was a new kind of animal. It also came in different shapes and sizes, but all sizes had sharp teeth. Alarm wakened in Princess's bones. Her legs went hard and bouncy and her short tail stuck straight up over her back.

"She's never seen a dog before!" Roland said. "I should have realized. My previous trainer had two, and the foals were used to them."

"She's not in a panic," the trainer said. His voice was slightly warmer than usual. "She sees that her mother doesn't care. I've gotta hand it to her—she's a smart little thing!"

He was right. Princess had already noticed that her mother was perfectly calm. None of the other ponies seemed concerned. Princess's tail lowered, her neck softened. She walked behind her mother with the trainer at her side toward a barn with a long row of stalls.

But wait, they were going inside? There was so much to see

out here! Princess twisted her neck to look back. Just then a space opened up between two ponies, and there was a—what? A small person. Young. A human foal? She had dark hair and wide, shining dark eyes that locked with Princess's own. She was just as excited as Princess. All this was new for her, too.

~

RAE tried to say, "Look! A foal!" But nothing came out. The dark foal's wide, shining eyes locked with hers.

Rae tugged Gammer's arm, since her voice didn't seem to work, and pointed.

Too late. The foal had already followed its mother into a stall. Gammer opened her program. "There are classes for mares and foals this morning. Let's go to the grandstand and get a seat, sugar-lamb. My feet think it's afternoon already!"

~

PRINCESS followed her mother into the strange stall. The old mare sighed. Tired. She began eating from the hay net. Princess paced, straining to hear and smell and understand. Who was whinnying? What made that unusual aroma? What was *happening?* Everyone smelled and sounded excited, especially Roland, who stood at the door talking to people and keeping them away.

Meanwhile, the trainer brushed Princess and her mother and polished their hooves. He put slim new halters on their heads and attached handsome new lead lines. The men looked at their watches.

"It's time," Roland said. He took the mare's lead line. The trainer took Princess's. The stall door was flung open wide, and Princess and her mother went forth into the new world.

RAE twisted in her seat, trying to see every pony on the showgrounds all at the same time. Gammer kept pointing out dogs. "Yes, yes," Rae said, turning her head, because there went a Fjord horse with its mane bristling straight up, and there was a lovely blond Haflinger—

The gate to the ring opened. A woman's voice came over the loudspeaker. "This is Abby Portchester, welcoming you to the Twelfth Annual Pleasant Valley Animal Shelter Benefit Horse Show. The first class of the day, pony mares with foal at side, please enter the ring now."

They were coming in. Fuzzy Shetland mares with foals like plush stuffed toys. Welsh mares with big bellies and delicate legs and foals like fairies. Extremely spotted mares with aggressively spotted foals. "Those are ponies of the Americas," Rae said when Gammer asked. "They're little Appaloosas."

There were quarter ponies with muscular rumps, dark Fell and Dales ponies, and—

"That's a tall one," Gammer said, pointing to a gray mare. "I'd call that a horse, actually."

"It's a Connemara," Rae said. "They're the tallest pony. Adults ride them."

"Really!" Gammer said. "And do you like them? To me a pony is short and fat and . . ."

Gammer's voice went on, but Rae stopped hearing her. The Connemara mares were so sleek and beautiful, their foals so dark and wild-looking. They answered something in Rae, something deeper than even the feeling she had for the furry Shetlands.

"We're looking for one more pair," the announcer said. "The entry from Highover—no, here they come."

A fat old man walked into the ring, leading a beautiful silver-white mare. And beside the mare—

"That's the one," Rae said, as a gasp rustled through the crowd. "That's the one I saw . . ." This foal was different from the others, sturdy yet fairy-like, huggable yet proud, with an electric sort of presence.

"I can't stop looking at her," Gammer said.

Rae shook her head, agreeing. When a Shetland foal started bouncing around like a velvet rocking horse, she only glanced at it, then went back to watching the dark filly. The foal walked quietly beside the man leading her, but the way she stared at the Shetland made Rae realize—

"She wants to play!"

That wasn't what she was here for. How proudly the old mare and the old man walked! How insignificant, almost invisible, was the small man holding the foal's lead rope. People crowded close to the fence. The foal's tail flew up and her legs went springy. She wasn't actually afraid, Rae thought, just ready, as a foal must be if surrounded by predators. Her large eyes quested, seemingly searching for someone. Rae's hand came up. But that was silly. You didn't wave to a pony.

Soon they all lined up in the center. A woman with a clipboard looked closely at each one and made notes. Some foals' legs got fidgety. Their handlers walked them in circles. But Rae's foal posed beside her mother, both ponies gazing off over the crowd at the hills beyond.

"Which one will win?" Gammer asked.

40

"That one," Rae said, pointing to *her* foal. She had to win. And if she didn't, it didn't matter. That foal didn't need a blue ribbon to be perfect.

The judge sent the ringmaster off with her scores. He came back with a set of long, fluttering ribbons. The judge walked straight to the old mare, and everyone started clapping. The foal jumped and stared, while her mother bent her head graciously to let the judge put the blue ribbon on her halter.

After all the ribbons were awarded, the rest of the mares and foals left the ring. "Take a victory lap, Roland," said the announcer. "Give a cheer for a classic breeder, folks, and a very classy entry!"

People clapped, cheered, stood up, and many surged toward the mare and foal as they left the ring. The foal pranced, and the old man said, "Step back, folks. Give the little lady some air!"

The crowd divided in front of Princess and came back together behind her, following toward the stall. Rae was halfway out of her seat. "Can we—"

"Yes, let's see if we can get a closer look. I had no idea people did this at horse shows."

"They don't," said a lady sitting near them. "But Roland is a master showman, and that foal is something special."

There was a crowd around the stall door. Rae and Gammer were at the back of it, and the mare and foal were inside, out of sight.

The old man answered people's questions, his voice proud and joyful. Everyone wanted a look. He kept most of them back, but a few were allowed to come to the door and gaze. A sturdy old woman in a pink baseball cap looked for a long time.

"Beautiful, Roland," she said. It was the same voice that had come out of the speakers. "Absolutely beautiful. But beauty is as beauty does. These ponies are meant to be tough. Is she?"

The old man took a deep breath. "I don't know why she shouldn't be, Mrs. Portchester. She comes from tough stock."

"Pooh, Roland! Don't 'Mrs. Portchester' me just because I ask you a question. She's probably tough as nails. I hope she never has to find out."

She left, and a man who'd been standing with her said, "Are you interested in selling that youngster?'"

The old man seemed to swell to almost twice his size. "I've bred some fine ponies," he said. "But never one like this. I wouldn't take a million dollars for her."

A million dollars? *A million dollars?*

Rae turned away. They weren't going to be allowed to look over the stall door, and already a new class of ponies was going into the ring.

"You know that's a figure of speech?" Gammer said, as they walked back to their seats. "He's expressing how much she means to him."

Rae nodded, but she understood what Gammer may not have. It came to the same thing in the end. She could not fall in love with this foal. Any pony that had a chance of becoming *hers* would have to be a lot less perfect.

tides

"RAE, how's Eden?" Gammer asked, a few weeks into the summer. They were out delivering pies in the truck. "You haven't been to her house once since I got back."

"No," Rae said.

Gammer looked away from the road. "Anything wrong?"

Unexpected tears stung the backs of Rae's eyes. She turned to look out the window. "She sold Woolly Bear." Woolly Bear was a red Shetland with a black mane and tail. Rae had loved him since kindergarten, since the first day she found out that Eden loved ponies too. She'd visited Eden at least once a week after that, and they spent most of their time in the backyard with Woolly Bear. They groomed him, kissed him, sat on him, tumbled off—not learning much about how to ride, but learning a lot about courage. Meanwhile Woolly Bear did exactly as he chose: dozing, rolling on the grass, pounding along at his sewing-machine trot, or stopping fast and jolting them off. Eden's backyard had practically been Rae's second home. And now it wasn't.

Gammer said, "People do sell ponies. That's how other people get to buy them. He's pretty small, as I remember. Did he go to a place with little children?"

"Yes." Woolly Bear had a new family with three young children and a fourth on the way. It would be years before they outgrew him. It wasn't the worst thing in the world for Woolly Bear. "She rides at a stable now," Rae said.

"And that means you can't be friends?"

Rae didn't know how to answer. It wasn't just Eden riding at a stable—though that kind of riding was expensive, and not sharable with a friend who didn't take riding lessons. But before, they were the same, and now they were different from each other. Or maybe it was Rae's fault. She'd loved Woolly Bear too much, and Eden got jealous, and it didn't feel good to be together anymore.

"There are tides in friendships," Gammer said. "I hope this tide comes back in soon. You're a bit too solitary, lovebug. Sometimes I wonder if I'm doing wrong by going south in the winter. Maybe I should stay here and make sure you get out more."

"If you stayed, then I'd want to be home with you!"

It was a joke, but it was also true, and part of what made summers wonderful. Once school was out, Rae went everywhere with Gammer, delivering pies, talking and singing songs, playing word games, and keeping an eye peeled for ponies. Whenever they saw one in a roadside field, they stopped the truck. Whenever they saw a stable or a farm, they investigated. Elegant Briarwood, a hunter-jumper barn. Singin' Saddles, which was all about quarter horses and Western riding. The place that taught centered riding and the boarding stable at the edge of town and the Morgan farm.

~

When school started in the fall, Gammer was still home and she asked about Eden again. It was hard for Rae to talk about. She and Eden said hi to each other, but they didn't eat lunch together anymore, or gallop around the playground during recess, or sit drawing pictures of ponies on rainy days. Once a week Eden came to school in riding pants, the kind Rae's mother used to wear. Those were the days she had her lessons at Briarwood, the hunter-jumper barn. It had been the fanciest of all the horse farms Rae and Gammer visited. Lesson days were the hardest days to say hi on.

There were other kids in class that Rae liked, but they weren't friends the way she and Eden used to be. None of them loved ponies—except Lara, who liked *pink* ponies and unicorns with glittery horns. Rae liked Lara, but she hated pink ponies and glitter. She liked Tia, but not dressing up dolls and making up stories about them. She liked Bo, but computer games were boring.

There were also kids Rae didn't like. Some of the boys weren't as nice this year as they used to be. Jeff had discovered that it was Rae's father who drove the garbage truck, and he liked to pretend that Rae stank. "She does not!" Eden said fiercely, every time she heard him say it. So Eden was still her friend, really, and not many people liked Jeff this year. Still, school was less fun than last year, and after Gammer went south, the days started to feel too long.

chapter 9

Gone

PRINCESS got used to trailers over the summer, got used to shows. A class and ribbons in the morning. Back into the ring in the afternoon, with other ponies of all ages. They'd come out with an even bigger ribbon, long and multicolored, fluttering on the old mare's bridle, and Roland carrying a silver bowl or cup, or some other gleaming trophy. They were champions; someone would ask to buy Princess, Roland would proudly refuse, and then the day was over. They'd get into the trailer again, and when they got out, they were home.

A few days later people who'd asked to buy Princess would visit, look at her longingly, then give Roland a slip of paper, and load one or two other ponies in a trailer. It happened over and over, all summer. Later, Roland always gave the trainer a check. "A little bonus for you and Darlene. Hard work breeds success, and the other way around. I know that."

"A labor of love," the trainer said, showing his teeth like a smile.

Between shows, Princess and her mother spent their days in the paddock. The old mare moved slowly. She was quite ancient. People were always surprised to hear her age, and even more surprised that she had produced such a fine foal.

Her mother might be slow, but Princess was learning to be fast. She raced around the paddock, bucking and kicking up her heels. She chased birds and jumped over shadows and watched other foals in the faraway pasture. If only she could get there! But the fence was high and strong. She had to have fun by herself. She whirled in tight circles, chasing her own short tail, a game the cat taught her. She raced her shadow. Sometimes her mother raced too, for a short distance, or stood with her head high and her ears back, looking as if she might. When Princess galloped herself into panting exhaustion, her mother was always there to run back to, approving and welcoming.

Often Roland was there as well. He liked everything Princess did. Even when she experimented with nipping, he only laughed and pushed her head gently away. "I may be round, but I'm not an apple, little girl," he said. "You behave yourself!"

The days got shorter and cooler. The other foals were separated from the mares and put all together in one pasture. They neighed for their mothers, and the mothers answered back.

Where are you?

Here! Where are you?

There was a loud afternoon, a shrill and sleepless night, and another day occasionally pierced by whinnies. Then the foals forgot, roving their large pasture in gangs and playing wild games. They were growing up. They already knew how to eat grass and hay. They didn't need milk, and they had one another for companionship. In another pasture the mares got down to serious grazing, to feed the new foals growing in their bellies.

Princess, too, was growing up. But Roland put off her weaning week by week, while the trees turned color and frost nipped the grass. "She's the old lady's last foal," he told the trainer. "Let's just let them stay together a bit longer."

The wind drove in cold from the north. The leaves fell from the trees. The grass stopped growing.

One afternoon the old man came to the fence as usual. At the sound of his voice, Princess's mother turned and trotted toward the fence.

And fell.

She never even stumbled. One moment she was up. The next she lay on the grass, not moving. Princess stood sniffing her mother's side, sweet-scented, familiar, and still. Roland hurried over, wheezing, and brushed his hand across her open eye. It never blinked.

"Gone." Slowly he straightened and looked off over the hills. "I hope I go that easily when my time comes. But poor Princess!"

The trainer put on the halter and led Princess into the stall, alone. Her mother didn't follow. Princess neighed, but her mother didn't answer. Again and again she didn't answer. Princess reared to look over the stall door, and the trainer shut the top half, leaving her alone in the dark.

Her mother had always been there, or if she was around

the corner out of sight, she had always answered. Something was wrong. There was a hole in the world and a huge empty hole inside Princess. She was afraid to even whinny. She stood perfectly still, straining to hear and see and understand.

After a while the men came back. Princess went to Roland, pressed her head against his chest. Safe in the shelter of his warmth and scent, she closed her eyes. "I'm sorry, little girl," he said. "So sorry." His warm hands rubbed her. She felt a little safer. Only a little.

"Bring a chair," he told the trainer, and when the chair came, he sat down. There he stayed, saying kind words or just being quiet, while Princess paced, and listened, and paced. The cat dropped in and experimented with lap-sitting. Darlene brought coffee, later a sandwich, and finally blankets.

"Are you really going to stay all night?" she asked. "She'll be all right. It's only another kind of weaning."

"The other foals were together," Roland said. "They could call to their mothers, and their mothers called back. Princess doesn't have anyone but me. My fault. I didn't see this coming."

He didn't see, either, the calculating look the woman gave him as she closed the stall door, and he didn't hear what she said to her husband in the privacy of the small house. "What *I* see coming, Charlie, is a crisis. That mare wasn't the only old thing around here."

Her husband looked at her warily and said nothing.

In the barn, Princess stopped pacing. She was exhausted, but she didn't lie down, just stood listening, waiting for morning and her mother.

sam and tully

PRINCESS'S mother didn't come in the morning. She never came.

Winter came instead, a hard winter. The air was cold. Wind blew across the mountains, driving pellets of snow. The trainer blanketed Princess and gave her special vitamins, but she didn't thrive. Her coat lost its gloss. Her ribs showed. She looked almost ugly, and inside she felt ugly, dull, and hopeless.

The vet came to look at her. He found nothing wrong, nothing physical. He and Roland quarreled. "For heaven's sake," the vet said. "Turn her out with the other weanlings. She's starved for companionship! She needs other ponies."

"It's too late. They don't know her, they'd gang up on her—"

"And she'd get over it! Ponies are tough! You're treating this one like a porcelain doll. You're afraid she'll get scuffed or dirty! And yourself, too. You're turning into an eccentric old loner,

Roland, living way up here in your castle. Get out! See people!"

"People are a mixed blessing," Roland said in a hard voice Princess had never before heard from him. "Sometimes they give you advice you haven't asked for!"

"Someone has to!" the vet said.

Roland did not respond. When the vet was gone, he asked the trainer, "Do you know how to give shots, Charlie?"

"I've done it," the trainer said, sounding wary.

"You're going to do a lot more of it. I won't have that fellow back on the place, not unless there's a real emergency."

Princess was not an emergency. There was nothing wrong with her that a veterinarian could help. But some things did help. The cat came most nights and curled up on her back to warm his toes. His purr and body heat pressed through the blanket and made her feel . . . not good, but better.

She felt better, too, when Roland was there. He spent hours with her, though the cold air didn't improve his health. He wore a warm coat and scarf, and a bright red wool hat with a pom-pom on the top. Still, his breathing changed after a few minutes outdoors. He coughed frequently, and the trainer's wife often wondered aloud why he didn't winter in Florida. "We'll look after things here," she said.

"Princess needs me," he always answered.

"He's out there talking to her," she reported to her husband one morning. "He's telling her stories, just as if she were a child!"

Not exactly. The old man fed Princess sugar lumps out of his hand, not ordinary white cubes, but lumpy golden-brown ones, the kind that fancy restaurants served. He rubbed her neck, and he apologized.

"The name brought bad luck. I didn't mean it that way. It just seemed right—but princesses lead difficult lives. It's lonely at the top. If I'd turned you out with the rest of them, you and your mother, things would be different now. But I couldn't bear to, and . . . well, let's get through this winter, and we'll see what spring brings."

～

RAE'S class welcomed two new students after February vacation, Sam and Tully, twins. Sam's red hair hung on each side of her face like ironed curtains. Tully's red hair curled and bounced and frizzed. Sam had brown eyes. Tully had green eyes. Everybody wanted to be friends with them, but at lunch the first day, they asked Rae to sit with them.

"You don't talk as much as everybody else," Tully said. "We think that's interesting. So—here's what you need to know about us."

Sam said, "We have plans. I'm a writer."

"And I'm going to be a scientist," Tully said.

A writer? A scientist? Rae loved books, but she didn't imagine writing them. She liked knowing all about ponies' bones and minds and insides, but most science had nothing to do with ponies.

But she liked Sam and Tully anyway—or thought she was going to—and they were waiting for her answer. "I'm going to have a pony," Rae said. Her face got hot. It wasn't the same thing, was it? Now they both were looking at her, heads tilted.

"Why a pony?" Sam asked.

"Not to be critical," Tully said. "But a pony's just a little horse, right?"

"A kiddie version," Sam said. "Why don't you want a real horse?"

It was a question Rae was asked often. Each time, she stumbled over the answer. Now, with Sam's brown eyes and Tully's green eyes watching her, she dug deeper.

"Because—look, people think ponies are cute and not serious. But ponies are tough! They live longer than horses. They get fat on hardly any food. They're fast and strong, and they have a different kind of mind. Ponies don't panic. They *think*. They take care of themselves. A horse is like an overgrown pony. Thinned out, kind of."

"Like punch after the ice cubes melt," Tully said. "Okay. We get it."

"When you have your pony, what will you do with it?" Sam asked.

"Take . . . care of it?" Rae said. That was a thin answer. It didn't explain why *I'm going to have a pony* was the first thing she'd wanted them to know about her. She did want to ride her pony. It was important. But not the most important thing. Having, living with, knowing, loving—that was what it was about.

"It's simple," Tully said. "She'll be complete. We all have something we're hungry for. I want to know things. You want stories. And Rae has a lost pony twin somewhere. When she finds it, she'll finally be her whole self."

"Are you *sure* you're not the writer?" Sam asked. "Because that's a great story!"

Sam was right. What Tully had just said was Rae's true story, said in a way she had never thought of before. Nobody had ever understood her as well or as fast as Sam and Tully did.

"The thing is, we can't afford a pony yet," she said. "It might be a long time—and what if I get too tall?" It was her greatest fear.

They looked at each other, a twinny thing they did. "I need to meet your family," Tully said. "Ask us over to your house."

When that happened, a few days later, Tully looked Dad over. She asked to see photo albums. "Is that your mother?" she asked. "Are those your cousins?"

The next Monday at school she announced, "Good news! I've been studying the genetics. There's almost no chance of you getting tall. Your family is all small, especially the women."

"Thank you," Rae said. Gammer had hinted as much, but without the backup of science.

"Do ponies come in different sizes?" Sam asked. "What's the biggest a pony can be?"

Rae explained that ponies had to be smaller than fourteen and a half hands. Then she explained that a hand was four inches. Tully did the math. Fifty-eight inches.

"—and that's at the withers," Rae said. "The part of a pony's back, just behind the neck."

"And fifty-eight inches is okay?" Sam asked. "Or do ponies get less good as they get bigger?"

"Bigger is better, if you can only have one," Rae said. "If I get a big pony, I never have to outgrow him."

"And he's a him?" Sam asked. "Does it have to be a boy?"

"I always say him," Rae said.

"So he's a boy," Tully said. "Fancy? Or not so fancy?"

"We can't afford fancy," Rae said. "I'll fancy him up by the way I take care of him. Like Dad. He makes sculptures out of things people throw away—"

"Wait, those sculptures are made out of trash?" Sam said. "I knew they were cool, but I didn't know they were that cool! You have to invite us to your house again!"

"Besides—pie," Tully said. "When does your grandmother get back?"

"In the spring," Rae said.

Which came sooner than she expected this year. Time went faster when there was someone to read books with, and do chemistry experiments with, and educate about ponies. Tully and Sam were town girls. "I don't see us riding, ever," Sam said. "But we want to know all about it, because ponies are your art."

"And your science," Tully said.

"Yes," Rae said. "Thanks."

chapter 11

spring

PRINCESS hadn't known that winter wasn't forever, that the days would get longer and warmer again, the winds softer, sweet-smelling. But they did. The snow disappeared, grass grew, birds came back to build nests in leafy branches, and foals were born. From her paddock Princess watched them take their first wobbly steps, grow steady and brave, and learn to run. But inside her, the ice didn't thaw, the days never brightened.

Roland fretted. "She hasn't gotten over it. She's too quiet."

"Put her out with the other yearlings," the trainer suggested.

Roland turned slightly pale. "You know we can't do that. They were pasture raised. She's grown up alone. She could be hurt."

"Put a couple of yearlings in the next paddock, then," the trainer suggested. "They can play across the fence."

That very afternoon Olive and Frankie moved in next door,

two rough and shaggy pasture ponies who'd never spent a night in a stall. Bright-eyed and wary, they stood close together at the other edge of the paddock and looked at Princess, who stretched her neck high to peer far over the fence and gaze hungrily at them.

Olive, the bolder one, stepped forward. She and Princess bowed their necks. Their pricked ears almost touched. Olive's warm, grassy breath flowed over Princess's face, tickling.

From deep inside Princess a sound burst forth, one she'd never made before—a huge mare squeal. One front hoof struck out—she didn't even know why. Olive squealed and struck too. Then they sniffed again, squealed again, and raced along the fence to the very ends of their paddocks, turned, and raced back.

The old man dabbed at his eyes. "She hasn't played since her mother died. Thank you, Charlie. I . . ." He fumbled in his pocket, the one where he kept his checkbook.

"No," the trainer said. His wife dug him in the side with one of her long, pointed nails, but he looked away.

Olive and Frankie knew nothing of the wider world, but they knew about playing, and they taught Princess. Soon she, too, could make eye contact, toss her head, swish her tail, and start a race or a mock fight.

What she couldn't do was scratch shoulders. Olive and Frankie scrubbed each other's withers with their teeth, tangled and braided each other's manes. It made Princess feel itchy and alone. But all the fences at Highover were what the old man called Connemara-tall, to keep in a herd of natural jumpers. It was possible to reach between the boards, but awkward. When wither-scratching happened, Princess could only watch.

Still, the ponies could say things to each other, they could play, they could stand next to the fence in a dozing threesome.

It helped. Princess's heart warmed and thawed. Her winter coat shed out and she turned glossy and smooth, nearly black with big silver dapples. Her large dark eyes watched the world in a slightly worried way. Her legs were as slender and steely as a deer's.

Judges adored her, as a dark yearling, as a gray two-year-old. The tack room glittered with silk ribbons and silver cups. Buyers followed her home from shows, ponies went away in trailers, and the trainer pocketed one fat bonus after another.

"Pretty sweet," he said one evening. "The better Princess does, the better we do."

"He can afford more," his wife answered. "Sitting all alone in that enormous house, on his pile of money. It isn't right."

"Not right? Why isn't it right? There have to be rich people, so poor people like us have somebody to work for."

"That is a very limited way of looking at it, Charlie. But I agree, it's important to be near the rich—my favorite kind of people. They're so unobservant."

rusty

RAE, meanwhile, joined the writing contest at school with Sam, and did a science fair project with Tully. She picked berries with Gammer in the summer, apples in the fall, rhubarb in the spring—and back to berries again, as another whole year passed. Her bank account grew and so did she, but not excessively. Tully had been right.

Though Rae and her bank account grew, the back lawn did not.

At least it didn't shrink. Dad kept himself from planting fruit trees there, or even potatoes. "I'm holding that space open for your pony," he said, "when the time comes."

And when would that be? Rae didn't ask. She joined the 4-H horse club in the neighboring town instead. You could join even if you didn't have a horse or pony and compete in the quiz bowl and in judging contests. The leader held classes with the kids who did have horses, on things like grooming and health care. It was a chance to be near horses and ponies, and it helped.

Dad heard Rae not asking. He was very busy in his shop in the days leading up to her tenth birthday, and on her birthday morning, he asked her to come out with him. Alone.

Rae looked across the table at Gammer. She must know what this was about, but her face didn't tell Rae anything. She followed Dad outdoors.

"You might hate this," he said as they walked across the yard. "If you do, just tell me, and we don't have to mention it to anybody."

What could it be? Rae felt her heart stutter as she entered the shop half of the barn. Her whole life she'd dreamed of coming out here and meeting her pony for the first time. This was not that dream. Still—

Dad switched on the light.

It *was* a pony. Not a real pony—but a pony, life-size, one of Dad's sculptures. Round tractor headlights made wild, goggly eyes. Wire broom bristles stood straight up for a mane. The well-sprung ribs were made from an old hay rake, and the madly galloping legs were made of fence posts and pistons and who knows what. Bolted onto its back was a real saddle.

"Do you hate it?" Dad asked.

Rae put her hand on the smooth seat of the saddle. The pony almost seemed to cock his head at her, inviting her to get on.

"I thought you could sort of ride," Dad said. "After you read your books . . . you could practice. But if you hate it—"

"No," Rae said. Dad was feeling bad about his present, and she hated *that*. But this pony—

"I'm going to call him Rusty," she said. "Can you help me get on?"

"He's not very steady yet," Dad said. "I'm going to mount him on a big spring so we can put him out in the front yard. Here—I'll steady him, and you can get on."

Rae put her left foot into the stirrup and swung her right leg over Rusty's back. She settled into the saddle and looked out between Rusty's two swiveling ears (made from garden trowels). She felt like crying, and she felt like laughing.

"I love you, Dad. And I love him. Let's put him in the backyard."

"Oh, because that's the pony pasture?"

"No, because I'm going to ride him," Rae said. "Just not out by the road where everybody can see."

~

This year Sam and Tully came to the horse show with Rae and Gammer. They didn't go on the first day, the breed show, because Gammer was making pies for a wedding. Instead they went on the third day, which turned out to be completely different. Instead of polished adults and purebred ponies, the ring was full of kids, some skillful, some really not. The 4-H kids, who mostly rode Western, knew just what they were doing. So did the hunt-seat riders from Briarwood stable. Including Eden. Rae spotted her right away, but didn't mention it.

Other kids had more trouble. Ponies ran away with helpless riders, or stopped still and refused to move. Kids fell off and got up laughing, or tried to.

Sam said, "So this is what riding looks like before people get good—oh look, isn't that Eden? From our class?"

Rae nodded. It was hard not to feel jealous, seeing her on a handsome dark pony, riding extremely well. "*She's* good."

"This is what you should be doing," Tully said.

"Yeah, why don't you get lessons?" Sam asked. "Then you'll be ready when you actually get your pony. I mean—4-H helps, but it looks like there's a ton to learn."

"Yeah, about gravity!" Tully said.

They were right. Rae hadn't realized it till this moment. She'd been working too hard at not asking, at learning all she could from books and 4-H. But this was another way. She should be out there, falling off and struggling, laughing and learning. She didn't need a pony of her own to do that.

"You're wise young women," Gammer said. "I'm going to go scout, and see if I can meet some of the people teaching these youngsters. You three stay here where I can find you."

She came back looking pleased. "See that woman helping that group of kids over there?"

"With the red pony?" Rae asked. He was named Radish, and he checked every important pony box—round, cute, fast, smart, and extremely naughty.

"Those kids don't look as fancy as some of the others," Sam said. "They're getting ribbons, though."

"Yes. That's Tish. She runs a riding stable on the other side of our mountain. I don't have customers on that road, so that's why we haven't been there yet. We'll go over there as soon as I have time, and check it out. It might be the kind of place where lessons are affordable."

When they visited a week later, it seemed that Gammer might be right. Rae loved the old barn and the way the tops of the half doors were worn smooth by generations of horse necks. She loved the dozen horses and ponies, none outstandingly beautiful, all wise and full of character. She loved the battered ring. She loved Radish.

Lessons, unfortunately, were not affordable enough.

"I can only manage three this summer," Gammer said. "That's nowhere near what you should have—but now I know what to budget for."

Three lessons seemed like a lot to Rae. Aside from playing on Woolly Bear, she had only ever ridden pony-ride ponies, for five minutes at a time at the fair. This summer she had three whole hours, each on a different pony, and by the third time she actually got to trot. "You're making great progress!" Tish told her after that lesson. "Keep up practicing on your own."

Rae nodded. After each lesson she'd gone straight home and ridden the whole lesson again on Rusty, trying to remember everything she'd learned. That must be what Tish was talking about. Rae kept that up all fall, until it was too cold to be sitting outdoors on a pony made mostly of cast iron. *Sit straight and relaxed. Heels down and back. Elbows at your sides.*

Sometimes she imagined a fairy godmother touching Rusty with a wand and bringing him to life. He was exactly the kind of pony she would have someday, scrappy, feisty, and not very beautiful, but with a spine of steel.

open
house

PRINCESS was playing with Olive and Frankie on the autumn day when an ambulance screamed up the long driveway to the farm and took Roland away. He didn't come back that evening, or the next morning. Princess watched the big house, listened for his footsteps, and began to freeze inside.

The third morning he did come. His hand with the brown sugar trembled, and his voice was thin. The trainer stood by his elbow, watching him like the cat at a mouse hole, and from a distance the woman watched them both.

"A warning, they tell me," Roland said. "It's time for me to consider what I want to do with my ponies. Time for a dispersal sale."

"Everything must go?" the trainer asked. "Even this one?"

"Not Princess. And not the older mares, or the ones who'll have difficulty finding good homes. It's a tough world out there for undesirable ponies, and I have the means to keep them here. There will still be a position for you, Charlie, if you care to stay. Princess will need to be trained, and I'd like to campaign her under saddle. The culmination of all my work—I want to get her out there for the world to see."

The trainer nodded, with a wary glance at his wife. "All right. We'll get things ready for a sale."

Roland looked around him. "I've never opened this place to the public, and now it's almost too late. Let's hold an open house the morning of the sale. Let everyone come, not just people with money in their pockets."

RAE pressed her nose against the window of Gammer's truck as they climbed the hill, winding up between deep, dark woods. "Highover," Gammer said. "Boy, they aren't kidding!"

"Look!" Sam and Tully said together. Sam pointed at the cupola of a barn, peeking over the shoulder of the hill above them. "A pony weather vane!"

"The real thing!" Tully pointed at the green field they were passing. It sloped down to trees and a brook, with a three-sided shed for shelter and a high board fence.

Rae was hanging out the window now. The field was full of ponies. They weren't especially fancy-looking, more like the Connemaras she had seen in pictures, running half wild on the Irish moors. A bit of hope snuck into her heart. This was a sale, after all. Was it possible there were ponies here that no one else would want? Ponies a person like her could afford?

"Why are the fences so high?" Tully asked. "I mean—talk about overkill!"

"Connemaras are good jumpers," Rae said. "The fences have to be high."

They swept around a curve and there was the big house, tall and grand like a castle, and a second house that was only small by comparison. The barn was like a Victorian palace, with a wide, open door and a gleam of brass within. The Irish flag flew over a large white tent, and there were crowds everywhere, even though Gammer had gotten them here quite early.

Gammer found a place to park far out in a field, and they walked back. "There's Eden," Sam said. Rae nodded, hardly hearing. She was on the lookout for more ponies.

A moment later someone said, "Well hello, Rae!" It was Tish. She had a tall boy with her whom she introduced as her nephew Bill. "Not a pony person," Tish said. "He's starting a long bike ride from here, as soon as he checks out the refreshment table!"

Bill edged into the crowd around the long table and emerged with several doughnuts in his large hands. He gave them each one and ate the last himself, in two bites. "Mmm. Cinnamon. Have fun, Aunt Tish. Don't raise your hand and accidentally buy a pony!" He tightened the strap on his helmet, stepped onto his bike, and disappeared down the long hill.

"What a crowd!" Tish said. "A lot of us locals came to gawk, I guess. The people with real money will be here this afternoon, for the auction."

The doughnut went dry in Rae's mouth. The word *money* tended to do that to her. She headed into the barn. Ponies looked over stall doors, framed in gleaming brass grilles. They looked friendly and curious, and some were strikingly handsome. Everything looked like a picture in an expensive catalog—even the cross-ties on the walls of the aisle made Rae want to reach out and touch them. Every halter on a Connemara head was rich, soft leather, and the lead ropes were made of braided leather.

Down at the far end of the aisle, the tack room was even more crowded than the refreshment table. So many people were jammed in Rae could barely see through the door unless she stood on tiptoe. She glimpsed championship ribbons and silver cups, pony photos on the walls, and saddles, bridles, even harnesses, all perfectly clean and hung on racks. There was no getting in there, though, and the ponies were what Rae really wanted to see.

It wasn't possible to get close to them, either. Between every two stalls stood someone wearing a maroon Highover shirt, asking people to keep back. Rae obeyed, studying each pony in turn as she walked down the aisle. Could one of them be *her* foal, the dark filly she'd locked eyes with at the show? It might look very different now. Foals could change color dramatically as they got older. But Rae thought she'd know, and after walking the length of the barn, she was pretty sure that foal wasn't here.

The last stall had its top door closed. Squarely in front of it in a director's chair sat a large old man. Rae recognized him. He'd been at the show that day, leading the dark foal's mother. He'd been the one who said—

"Why is that door closed?" Sam wondered aloud—but quietly. The old man looked protective.

"Maybe the pony's nervous," Rae said. Some of them were. She could tell by the swiveling ears and flashing eyes. They weren't frightened exactly, just alert. And they should be. In a couple of hours someone else would own them, and they would leave this beautiful place forever.

"There are other ponies out in the paddocks near the tent," Gammer reported, coming into the barn. "Some foals, even."

As Rae moved in that direction, a man came up to the closed stall and said, "You won't reconsider? I've come all this way in the hope that you'd finally sell her."

Swelling where he sat, the old man said, "I wouldn't take a million dollars for her."

Sam and Tully exchanged a twin look, and each put a hand on Rae's shoulders. "I'm not sure this is a good place for you to be," Sam said. "Million-dollar ponies!"

Rae put an arm around each of them and squeezed herself into a twin sandwich. "I don't need a million-dollar pony. I need one like Rusty, only real."

"Some of those ponies down in the field looked pretty gnarly," Tully said. "Are they for sale too?"

Gammer said, "I'll ask—excuse me, ma'am?" She approached a handsome, dark-haired woman in a Highover shirt, who was standing near the barn door. "Are the ponies down in the field going to be sold?"

The woman turned her head and looked them over. Three kids. Gammer in her T-shirt that said *The Pie Lady*. "Not at this time," she answered.

～

PRINCESS listened to the voices beyond the closed door. So many. It was like a show, if the show had come here. She heard Roland talking proudly.

But as the morning ended, the voices faded, until there

was just one man in the distance talking fast and something pounding. One by one, ponies were led out of the barn. Even Olive and Frankie passed through. Princess heard the particular patter of their hooves on the floorboards, heard them blowing their breath out in their own distinctive snorts. They were not brought back. Princess began to hear hooves on trailer ramps and trucks starting. By the end of the afternoon, Highover was quiet and nearly empty.

And so it stayed. No more games and races. No more sniffing noses with Olive and Frankie over the fence or dozing together in the sun. Princess could see the field ponies, but they were far away. She didn't whinny to them. She knew. No one would let her go down there. Her life was here—the stall in the empty barn, the large paddock, the trainer's daily care, and the old man, coming every morning to give her brown sugar out of his hand.

chapter 14

the tiger's breath

PRINCESS had new things in her life that autumn as well. The time for serious training had begun. Circling on a lunge line. Wearing a saddle and bridle. Allowing the trainer to lean on her back. He was good at helping her understand what he wanted, and everything went smoothly. Roland watched every session and was pleased.

But one day the trainer's wife was there too, in riding breeches and a helmet, coming right up to Princess, putting her hands on her.

A shudder ran through Princess's body. She sidestepped, tucking her tail.

"Whoa!" the trainer said, sounding surprised. He gripped the bridle more tightly. "Try again." Once again the woman came close.

Every bone in Princess's body wanted to run. The woman

moved slowly, spoke quietly, made no obvious threat. But Princess remembered claws in her chest and the smell of blood.

The trainer held her. The woman mounted, and her weight settled into the saddle. "All set." Her voice came from behind Princess's head, where a tiger's breath would scorch as it opened its jaws for the killing bite. Where she'd felt it once before.

She thrust her head down, tearing the reins through the trainer's hands. "Darlene, *bail*," he shouted. His wife's feet slapped the ground; Princess bucked. It all happened at once.

He grabbed the reins again. "Darlene, are you hurt? I'm sorry! She caught me—"

"Strip the saddle off," Roland interrupted. In a moment his fingers were gently probing along Princess's spine. She dropped her head and breathed deep. She hadn't meant to buck. It just happened. But the woman was off her and standing several yards away, and that felt much better.

"Nothing seems to hurt her," Roland said. "Should we try again?"

"We'd probably better not let her get away with it. You game, Darlene?"

"Oh, I'm game!" the woman said.

But when she came forward, Princess backed up fast. The trainer went with her, not letting her pull on the reins. "Whoa!" he said breathlessly, and, as there was enough distance between her and the woman, Princess stopped.

"I don't like this," Roland said. "We haven't had a bit of trouble with her up till now. What's going on, Charlie?"

The trainer didn't answer directly. "I guess it had better

be me that gets on her. I weigh a little more, but—maybe she likes me better."

"Try it. Let's see if we can find a good note to end on."

The trainer spent a few moments stroking Princess, readjusting the saddle and bridle, soothing her. She needed that. Her legs felt jangly and her back had a tight hump in it, right under the saddle. What would happen next?

"Sir, if you'd stand at her head?" the trainer said. "Don't try to hold her!"

Princess stood with her head close to Roland's chest, breathing his scent. From the back corner of her eye she watched the trainer. What was he up to? He gathered her reins in his left hand, put his left foot in the stirrup. Stepped down and patted her. Did it again.

Next he put his weight in the stirrup. Princess stood still. He stepped up-down, up-down, then up all the way, swinging his right leg over her back, sitting in the saddle.

He was heavier than his wife, and this was all new. But it was him, not her. No urge to buck gathered along Princess's spine. She waited to see what would happen next.

"Step away from her head, sir. Please." Roland backed up. With gentle pressure on one rein, the trainer turned Princess to the left. She took a few steps, then a few more, and soon she was carrying him around the ring.

It felt awkward and unbalanced, as if she'd forgotten how to walk. But she circled the ring at his request, back to Roland. "Whoa," the trainer said. It was a word he'd taught her well. Princess stopped. "Let's quit while we're ahead," he said, and his weight lifted out of the saddle, and the sugar came out of Roland's pocket.

"*That's* my Princess. She looked beautiful, Charlie. But we're seeing the fruit of that unfortunate episode the first day. Will she fear all females? That would be a problem."

He watched the next training sessions closely, as the trainer showed Princess how to lower her neck, lift her back, and let the power of her hindquarters swing through. Within a few weeks she was carrying him confidently at a trot and then a canter, building strength, improving her balance.

One day a teenager named Marie arrived, helmeted, booted, and ready to ride. "As I explained over the phone, we think Princess may be afraid of females," Roland said, while Marie patted Princess, and Princess sniffed her politely. The trainer had good reason not to comment on that, and it took Roland a while to notice.

"Huh!" he said, when it finally dawned on him. "Mount up, then. Let's see what happens."

Marie seemed tense as she climbed into the saddle. Princess was tense too. She tipped one ear back, wondering what was going on. "So far so good," the old man said, stroking Princess's neck. "Walk her around a little."

Princess and Marie circled the ring. Marie felt a bit clumsy up there, but Princess soon found the trick of carrying her.

"So it's about you, Darlene," Roland said. "I guess you won't be showing her. Just as well. You have a heart of gold, my dear, but nothing brings in the ribbons like a pretty young face. We're such old friends, I know you won't mind me saying that."

The trainer's wife did mind, very much, but as they were not in fact friends she said nothing; just shot a look at him, hard and stinging as a small pebble. This was not the kind of insult she would forget.

~

Throughout that fall and early winter, the trainer worked with Princess. Roland loved to watch, and the woman often joined him. He seemed to like her. He liked both of them. But it didn't escape Princess's notice that the cat never rubbed around their ankles. He appeared only when Roland or Princess were alone.

She was alone again that winter, after the ambulance came a second time. Everything in the barn continued as usual, yet the days felt empty until, a week later, Roland returned, walking with a cane, speaking more slowly, breathing with a deeper rasp. No lights came on in the upper part of the house anymore. The trainer and his wife argued about that when no one was listening.

"He only uses those two downstairs rooms," Darlene said. "He'd never notice anything missing."

Charlie said, "You know I want you to have everything you deserve, but it's too dangerous. We have no reason to go in the house. If we were caught there, what would we say?"

"I'd think of something. He won't last forever, and he won't need a trainer much longer, either. We need to think ahead—"

At that moment Roland walked into the tack room with the cat in his arms. On seeing the pair, the cat vaulted onto a high shelf and wrapped his tail around his paws.

"Should you be coming down here so often?" the wife asked,

pulling out a chair for the old man. "I'm afraid you're not taking very good care of yourself. If you like, I could fix a dinner for you when I make ours, and bring it up on a tray."

"That's very kind of you," Roland said. "Perhaps I'll take you up on that."

Behind his back the trainer raised his eyebrows and gave her an admiring look. The cat licked one gray wrist and kept his own counsel.

chapter 15

eden

RAE held up her hand to stop Sam from talking. Without turning her head, or stopping chewing her sandwich, she listened. The cafeteria was loud, but Eden's voice still penetrated.

"No matter what I tried, I could *not* land on the right lead after a jump. But yesterday I finally got it!"

The right lead. Eden was talking about riding. Again. Lately she'd started sitting at a table near them at lunch, talking about horses and jumping in a very overhearable voice.

Rae swallowed and pointed with her eyes. Sam nodded. "Fourth time. Not an accident."

"She needs you to hear," Tully said. "Who else understands? Or cares? Look at poor Lara!"

". . . and it feels *amazing*," Eden was saying. "It's like I'm part of him all of a sudden. We're airborne, and then we touch down and his legs are already organized . . ."

How could you be airborne over a jump and already know exactly how you and the pony would land? "How did she do it? I missed that part?" she asked. Sam and Tully shrugged.

This was an opportunity, Rae realized. Wasn't Gammer always talking about noticing opportunities? In this whole room, full of people she'd known all her life, Eden was the one person who cared about what Rae cared about, and knew something about it. "I'm going over there," Rae said. "Be right back."

She took her lunch to Eden's table. Eden wasn't shocked to see her sit down. She'd made this happen. Rae decided not to mind that.

"How did you get the right lead?" she asked. "Sorry, I wasn't eavesdropping, but—I didn't hear that part." She had never cantered on a pony—yet. She didn't feel the need to share that, but she wanted to learn.

"It's all about how you set them up for the jump," Eden said. "You know—your approach?"

Rae had never jumped a pony either, but she nodded in a tell-me-more way. Lara slipped away, and Rae fell into a new world. Riding lessons twice a week. At Briarwood. Competitions. Ribbons. This was amazing!

"She asked me to go watch a lesson!" she reported to Sam and Tully, who gave each other one of those twin looks.

"Girl's gotta do what a girl's gotta do," Sam said.

"You know where to find us," Tully said—like Rae was going somewhere.

The next day she walked out of school with Eden, wearing a pair of Mom's old riding pants that was just starting to fit her and short boots with heels. She could ride in these, if anybody asked her.

"Hello, Rae," Eden's mother said when they got into the car. "It's nice to see you!" *After such a long time*, were the words she didn't say. Rae snuck a look at Eden and saw Eden sneaking a look at her. It *had* been a long time, and it felt a little awkward. But all they needed was a pony to change that.

Eden's mother drove them to Briarwood. It had been a while since Rae had visited it with Gammer, and when she walked in, it felt like the barn up at Highover: bright pine boards, new grilles on every door, expensive blankets folded just so on their hangers. Nothing was mended with duct tape or baling twine. The horses and ponies here deserved perfection and got it.

In a moment she was being introduced to Guillaume, Eden's French Saddle Pony. Rae hadn't known there was such a thing as a French Saddle Pony. Guillaume—it was pronounced *Gi-ome*—was dark brown, powerful, polite, and reserved. He let Rae stroke his neck, though, and the moment she did, she was in love. Really, deep down, she *did* love beautiful ponies. Really, deep down, she didn't actually want a scrappy, scruffy pony like Rusty. She told herself she did, and if she got one, she would love him absolutely—but a pony like Guillaume would be even better.

Eden rode Guillaume in a private lesson given by Kayla, a thin blond woman with a ponytail. Rae watched without looking away once, trying to take everything in. But it didn't matter if she missed something. On the drive back, Eden went over the whole lesson again, explaining what it felt like, and what she'd been thinking, and how much she was improving.

It was almost suppertime when they dropped Rae off, a chilly April evening. Rae went back behind the house and got on Rusty. Never had he seemed more rusted, more funky. She was almost embarrassed to be sitting on him, even with no one looking. Out there in the half darkness, she tried to reproduce the way Eden had ridden. *Look up. Heels down.* She'd known that forever, but pretending to be Eden, it made more sense. Her body came together from head to toe in one perfect unit.

What had the teacher said about elbows? *Close to your sides.* Tish said that too. In fact, a lot of what Kayla said, Rae had already heard from Tish, but it sounded different in a place like Briarwood.

"Oh, she's always after my elbows," Eden said the next day. "Come again on Thursday. You can video me. Mom gets bored."

girls

PRINCESS turned three that spring. Her winter coat had shed out to silver-white, with dark, round dapples. Her legs were black as wrought iron, her mane and tail dark pewter. "I wish I could freeze her at this stage," Roland said. "She'll never be more beautiful."

The suppers hadn't made him noticeably healthier. Still, as spring warmed, he came to the barn every day to watch Princess work. The trainer rode her, perfecting her understanding till she obeyed his lightest cues. Afterward there was brown sugar out of Roland's trembling hand.

Show season began. At the first show, Roland led Princess into the ring for the halter class as usual. "No, thank you, Charlie," he said, when the trainer offered to do it. "Let me do what I love in the time I have left." He could barely keep up with

Princess, even walking, and when the judge asked him to trot her, the watching crowd grew still and anxious.

"If you're up to it," the judge added.

"If I drop dead showing Princess, I'll die happy," Roland said, and he shambled away from the judge with Princess trotting at his side, straight and true. The crowd cheered. The ribbon was blue. Everything was normal.

But later the trainer put on Princess's saddle and bridle and led her to a smaller ring behind the barn. A girl waited, a trim blond teenager who said, "Wow!"

Roland beamed. "You must be Hilda. And this is Princess."

Hilda stretched out a hand. Princess sniffed it politely. Then Hilda got on.

Princess turned her head and they looked each other in the eye. Hilda seemed nervous, almost scared. Amazing! No one had ever been even slightly afraid of Princess. It made her feel large and kind. She stepped forward when Hilda asked, shifted smoothly from walk to trot, from trot to walk, from walk to canter. She pricked her ears and arched her neck, trying to show Hilda that everything would be okay.

"Wow!" Hilda said. "I thought you were just a pretty face, but—wow!"

Roland said, "She looks happier than when you ride her, Charlie!"

"Girls and ponies," the trainer said, with his near smile.

When Hilda got off, Roland said, "That was lovely to watch. You are certainly up to the job of showing Princess. Her first class is at eleven." And at eleven, carrying Hilda, Princess walked back into the show ring.

She was used to halter classes, where ponies walked quietly, stood still, and trotted one at a time. Now, when the announcer said "Trot," all the ponies trotted. When he said "Reverse direction," each pony made a small neat loop and circled the ring the other way. Princess had never been among other ponies moving fast. She couldn't help being excited and almost a little scared.

To Hilda, this was normal. She wasn't even slightly alarmed. Princess listened hard and did what she asked, and they came out of the ring with another blue ribbon.

Hilda rode Princess three more times, for two more blue ribbons and, at the end of the show, the multicolored streamer and the silver cup. When she rode out the last time Hilda was crying. Princess didn't understand. Nor did she understand the tight hug around her neck, or Hilda's choked voice saying goodbye. They'd had fun. They were friends. What was there to be sad about?

A couple of weeks later, there was another trailer ride. Princess usually stood perfectly still while traveling, but this time the ride seemed long and slow. She shifted her feet and banged against the side of the trailer. *Hurry!* When the ramp went down, she stepped out eagerly, looking around. She spotted the stalls and almost towed the trainer toward them. At her stall, a dark-haired teenaged girl waited.

"Hi, I'm Anne."

Princess sniffed Anne's hand politely, looking past her. Where was Hilda?

Roland chatted with Anne, and later she rode Princess in the practice ring. "Okay!" She tried to sound unimpressed, but Princess knew otherwise. Anne thought Princess was amazing—and Princess thought Anne was nice. Fun, really. An excellent rider. But where *was* Hilda?

She never came, and at the next show Anne didn't come. It was like that all through the first half of summer—at the end of every long trailer ride, a girl, but never the same girl twice.

They were delightful. The trainer, with his hands and legs and seat, always said, *Don't do that. Or that. Don't do anything except just exactly what I tell you.* The girls said, *Wow! What a wonderful pony. I'm so lucky to be riding you.* They felt fizzy and light on her back, like they were playing.

But they never came back. Girls seemed nice on the surface, but they were not to be trusted, and Princess paid less and less attention to them. She circled the ring obediently, doing everything she was asked, but she scanned the rail as she circled. She flared her nostrils, searching for Roland's scent. When she spotted him her heart lightened, and she sent a silvery neigh floating across the crowd.

He always ducked and hid. Princess wasn't supposed to whinny in the ring. It might cost her the blue ribbon. He would find a post or a truck to stand behind. Still, sometimes his scent drifted toward the ring, and he'd see Princess's nostrils flutter.

When Princess came out with her blue ribbon or her rainbow-colored championship ribbon, he would meet her at the gate. He'd give her brown sugar, congratulate her rider, and wait. Within minutes someone would approach and ask to buy Princess. He'd take a deep, happy breath and say, "No. I've raised a lot of good ponies, but never one like this. I wouldn't take a million dollars for her."

plan b

PRINCESS loved summer—the warm sun, the green grass, the unpredictable show schedule, even the girls, unreliable as they were. But the old man continued to weaken, so slowly it was hardly noticeable.

Then one morning, he didn't come. An ambulance came instead. The trainer followed it downhill in his truck and came back hours later, wide-eyed.

"This is the big one," he told his wife. "He's not coming back."

She stood up. "Time to execute Plan B."

The next day, Princess listened for the old man's footsteps. He'd always come back before, and while he was gone, things carried on as usual.

Now nothing was as usual. Morning came but breakfast didn't, not for hours. Eventually the trainer dumped a flake of hay in Princess's rack and glanced at her water bucket. Dust floated on the surface, but he didn't change the water and he didn't clean the stall, just rushed away on business of his own.

Days passed. Princess was never once brushed. She began to feel sweaty and itchy under her stable blanket. The back door of the stall was left open, day and night. Princess went indoors when darkness fell, but she didn't sleep. She watched and listened. This wasn't right. The door should be closed at night, the blanket should come off by day, she should have a good brushing, and the old man should come.

The trainer hurried up and down the aisle, carrying things, packing them in boxes—saddles and bridles, halters, braided lead lines, training equipment, blankets and bandages and veterinary supplies. Everything was the best and most expensive of its kind. Everything was in excellent condition. The trainer and his wife had spent many spare moments polishing this tack. "Now our hard work's going to pay off!" Darlene said.

She packed boxes in the small house and made trips to the large house. Princess could hear her moving around in upstairs rooms. Each time she came back carrying a basket full of small, fragile items, which she wrapped with care and packed in one of her boxes.

One afternoon she paused outside Princess's stall. Princess moved toward the open back door.

"You know what burns me?" the woman said. With the old man gone, she no longer bothered to be careful how she spoke. "That we can't turn a dollar on this pony! The work we've put into her over the years! The offers he's turned down! Are you sure we can't make some kind of a deal?"

"Impossible," the trainer said. "She's valuable because of

who she is. She's got papers and a show record, and she's his. We aren't him, and we can't sell her."

"Papers can be faked. I could do a lot to this animal with a few bottles of hair product. Not everybody in this business is honest, Charlie!"

"It can't be done—no, Darlene." He stepped between her and the stall door. The air tingled the way it did before a storm. "It's not the pony's fault," he said. "Don't take it out on her. I'll go a long way for you—look how far I've gone already!—but I won't go there."

"No?" The wife looked him in the face. As they locked eyes, Princess slipped out the back door of the stall and trotted to the farthest corner of her paddock. It wasn't far enough. The high, tight fence confined her as it always had. But out here she had room to run. If she had to, she could make herself very difficult to catch.

Apparently, there was no need. "You know how it is with me," she heard the wife say. "Growing up hungry, and that 'princess' thing . . ." He immediately began to soothe and cheer her, as their voices faded toward the tack room.

The strange new life went on—three days, five, a week. Flies buzzed in Princess's stall, attracted by the dirt. No one groomed her, and certainly no one visited morning and night. Asking "How's my Princess?" Holding out sugar lumps on his palm. Even the cat stayed away. Always distrustful of the trainer and his wife, he found this a good time to hunt elsewhere.

Meanwhile, phones rang and rang in the two houses. Occasionally the trainer answered. "Any improvement?" he'd ask. "Ah. Too bad! Yes, all under control here. Nothing to worry about."

"And as long as she believes that," he said when he hung up, "she'll stay away and give us the time we need."

"Who is she?" Darlene asked.

"A niece. She lives somewhere in the city. A bit of luck, really, that he isn't more of a family man."

The next day the feed store truck brought sacks of grain and many bales of hay. The driver had heard about the old man's illness and wanted to know how he was doing. The trainer just shook his head.

"Big delivery," the driver commented. "Didn't think he had that many ponies left."

"A few," the trainer said. "Under the circumstances, I want to be sure we have enough feed to carry them into the fall."

"Glad they've got somebody to look after them," the driver said, and drove away.

"And that takes care of the feed store," the trainer said. "They won't expect to hear from us for a while."

"Then it's time," said his wife.

The next morning, they brought two rental trucks and loaded them with everything they'd packed and more—the hay, the grain, even the bales of straw for bedding. They didn't take the ribbons, which were of no value, though they were made of silk. The wife wanted to take the silver platters, bowls, and cups, but her husband said, "Too easily traced. Half of them have his name engraved on them."

"And half don't."

"Still—too risky, Darlene. They could be traced back to us."

"You know best," she said.

Similarly, they didn't take any halters with nameplates, or Princess's green wool sheet with her name embroidered in one corner. They took only what could be easily sold.

Early the next morning, before the sun was up, the trainer came into the stall. Princess wasn't exactly afraid of him and not exactly unafraid. She hesitated, and before she could make a decision, he clipped a lead rope to her halter and walked her outdoors into a chilly mist.

Princess expected to be put in the trailer. But they went past the trailer, down the driveway to the field gate. The trainer took her blanket off. A shiver swept over Princess. It wasn't a cold morning, but she'd worn the blanket for a week now, and the change was sudden.

The trainer opened the gate, and the field came alive with ponies, galloping toward them, hooves rumbling, manes tossing like tall grass in the wind. They were the remnants of the old man's herd—retired broodmares, unattractive geldings, a few young animals that hadn't gone into training. Never groomed, rarely handled, tough as nails, they were half-wild, but with a well-learned optimism about people and grain pails.

Princess's heart lifted. Alone in the barn with the trainer and his wife, she'd almost forgotten there were still ponies on the farm. They swirled around the gate. The trainer's wife kept them back with a whip.

The trainer led Princess into the field. "You'll be fine," he told her. "Plenty of room, plenty of grass—and in a couple of weeks somebody will wonder why they haven't heard from us and come up to check."

"A couple of weeks?" his wife said. "A couple of months would be safer. We don't want to take any chances."

The trainer looked at the field measuringly. "A month at most," he said. "The grass will barely last that long."

His wife looked at the field too. She didn't smile—she rarely did—but one corner of her mouth sharpened briefly. She only said, "I'm sure you're right, Charlie. Come on. We'd better get going."

The trainer let go of Princess's halter and stepped back. Instantly she was surrounded by ponies, sniffing, squealing, pushing against each other.

Alone in the center of the milling throng, Princess stood rigidly still, breathing in their breath, controlling her own reactions as Olive and Frankie had taught her. She knew none of these ponies, though she'd heard their neighs, seen them in the distance, smelled their scent as it drifted across the hillside. Blinded by their nearness, distracted by stamping hooves and swishing tails, overpowered by scents and small pointed ears pricking and flattening, she paid no attention as the trainer closed the gate, as he and his wife walked away, as two yellow rental trucks glided quietly down the long driveway.

Only the cat, in the empty barn doorway, watched them go.

chapter 18

field ponies

In the field, the wild chase started when a pony nipped Princess from behind.

She should have stood still, at the very least. Better yet, she should have lashed out with her back feet, squealed, bitten someone—anyone, it wouldn't have mattered who. It would have shown them that she wasn't to be pushed around.

Princess didn't know that. Feeling herself bitten, she jumped, and the ponies in front of her shied out of her way. She burst through them and raced away with the whole herd thundering after.

What would happen if they caught her? Princess didn't know. She swooped down the hill, ducking under tree branches, swerving around big rocks. She was frightened, but not very frightened. She was faster than all of them. She raced alongside the fence, jumped the brook, and galloped uphill around the three-sided shed. Down again. Up again.

She wasn't the fastest anymore. Their legs were hardened from years of running and playing on this hillside. Hers were not. One more trip up the hill, and she had to stop.

The ponies swept around her, jostling, squealing, nipping, trying to figure out who could push whom around. Who was the boss?

It certainly wasn't Princess. She'd never bossed anyone in her life, not even Olive and Frankie. She'd pretended sometimes, but it was just play, and the fence had been between them. Nothing stood between her and these field ponies.

Princess kept her expression polite. When a pony made a threatening face, she took a step away from it. A small step, because no matter where she turned, there was another pony, another threat. Every second she expected to be kicked or bitten.

But the moment the ponies all knew they could boss her, they moved away, dropped their heads, and the air was filled with the sound of tearing grass. Princess tried to follow. The nearest pony raised its head and flattened its ears at her. She stopped. It went back to eating.

Stay outside the herd, she was being told. There were fences here too, invisible, but very real. Still, she was near ponies. So many ponies. Tails swishing, feet stamping, teeth cropping grass, all in a delicious cloud of pony scent. She was not alone, for the first time since her mother's death.

And there was unlimited grass. Princess snatched a mouthful and raised her head as she chewed, gazing around at this new world.

The sun made its long trip across the sky. When it was high

and hot, the ponies drifted uphill to the shed. They stood inside, out of the sun, away from the flies. Princess wasn't allowed in. She stood sweating, kicking at flies that bit her belly and legs. She had practically never been bitten before. Always she'd had a fly sheet, and her legs had been spritzed with the best herbal-botanical fly spray. Flies *hurt!* And she was thirsty, another new experience. She didn't see her water bucket anywhere.

Late in the afternoon, the ponies wandered downhill. Princess followed them into the trees. At the very bottom of the pasture, a small brook gurgled. The ponies walked into it to drink.

Never in her life had Princess drunk from anything but a bucket, her own bucket, with her name on it. But she could smell this water, cold and wild. She turned upstream, away from the group, and stepped cautiously closer. The ground gave way under her hooves. Perhaps it wasn't safe? But she had to drink. Ignoring the slide and squish beneath her, she lowered her head, pricking her ears in astonishment as a minnow flashed past. The water tasted of minerals and moss, maple leaves and hemlock needles. Princess had never tasted anything so good.

When she turned to come up the bank, the other ponies were close. Princess made herself small and still. She avoided looking at the others, gazing vaguely at the spaces between them. That seemed to make her invisible. She was allowed close, close enough to feel their body heat, closer than she'd been to any pony except her mother.

The nearest pony was a black gelding named Skip. He was

the least important pony in the herd, the one everyone else had pushed around until Princess came. Now he put his ears back and threatened to bite. Princess shrank her body away from his teeth, but moved her feet only slightly, shifting so they stood side by side, nose to tail. Skip swished his tail, brushing flies from Princess's face as her mother used to do. She swished back, as she used to then. But now instead of a short, stubby brush, she had a long, full, elegant tail that hissed when she moved it. Flies flew up, and Skip turned his head toward Princess with a contented sigh.

After a while Princess shifted position and shyly lifted her muzzle. She scrubbed her upper lip on Skip's hip. He scratched hers, raking vigorously with his teeth, saying, *Harder*.

A peaceful, rested feeling spread through Princess's body. Around them other ponies scratched, swished, dozed. Far up the hill, the buildings stood silent and empty, occupied only by birds and mice. The cat watched over the empty grain bin. A phone rang once. Then all was still.

After a long time, the sun began to set. Princess looked toward the gate. Never in her life had she spent a night outdoors. The old man or the trainer had called her in to supper in her own stall. Even in this last week, when nothing was done right in the barn, she'd gone inside on her own, keeping to her routine.

Today the sun went down without anyone coming from the house. A mist rose from the grass. Crickets sang, the moon came up, and bats flew squeaking through the dark air. Owls hooted.

Princess had heard these sounds all her life, from inside

the barn. Now she was outdoors, with only the sky for a roof. Around her the ponies grazed, then dozed, then grazed again, in a settled rhythm of their own. Princess did what they did, but even in mid-doze her eyes kept opening wide, her ears kept pricking, her head kept turning toward the big dark house.

money

RAE spent half that summer with an expensive cell phone in her hands, videoing Eden's lessons. There was less time to spend with Sam and Tully, less time to pick berries with Gammer, less pony money.

One day Gammer dropped in at Briarwood, on her way back from delivering pies. She watched Eden's lesson for a while, silently. But when Rae got home in the afternoon Gammer had questions.

"Has anyone offered you a chance to ride?"

"No. Not yet."

"Are you learning?" Gammer asked. "Are you enjoying yourself?"

"Yes!" How could she not be? She got to hose Guillaume down after his lesson, give him his treat, even lead him back to his stall. When she came home her hands smelled like horse.

She had manure on her boots. "I'm having the *best* time!"

But that night Rae couldn't sleep. Gammer's questions gave her that ache in her throat, the one she always got on her birthday when it turned out a pony was still out of reach. She got up and looked out the window at the barn. Knowing it was silly, she did her old trick, blurring her eyes, trying to paint Guillaume out there.

It didn't work.

Was she learning? *Was* she having fun?

I never want you to feel that you can't ask for what you want. Gammer had said that once, and the result was that Rae rarely asked for anything. In some ways she didn't have to. Her family knew her biggest need and did all they could to support her.

Also, she was older. She understood how things worked. How little money you could make driving a garbage truck or selling sculptures. How small the back lawn was, compared to the daily grass needs of a large pony.

Had she made any progress, in all these years? She was learning things watching Eden, more than she'd learned in 4-H. But she'd learned more at Tish's in those three lessons on an actual pony.

Could she ask? After all, it was a business. Briarwood didn't give lessons, even though that was the word people used. They *sold* them, and that should mean anyone could buy one.

She opened her top bureau and took out her bank statement. *You're the only kid I know who even knows what a bank statement is,* Tully said once. And Sam said, *Except us, because we know you.*

They were at camp right now—Tully at science camp, Sam

at an arts camp where she was working on a novel. They were both learning about what they loved—and so was Rae, right? But if this was an opportunity, it wasn't working out as well as she had hoped.

After Eden's next lesson she made herself ask the instructor, Kayla, "Could *I* have a riding lesson sometime? I can pay."

Kayla looked startled. "Do you know anything?"

"I've watched—"

"Watching isn't doing. Have you ever sat on the back of a horse or pony like the ones here?"

"N-no."

"It would be completely inappropriate," Kayla said. "You need to start at the beginning and work your way up. I'm sorry."

She turned away, and Eden whispered, "I can't believe you asked that!"

"Why?" Rae said. She felt hard inside, angrier than she could ever remember.

"Well—I mean, this is a high-end stable. She doesn't do beginner lessons."

"I'm not a beginner," Rae said—which wasn't true, but she didn't care right now. "I've watched a *hundred* of your lessons. I've paid attention. I could do it!"

Eden looked at her through narrowed eyes. "You made up with me because you thought you'd get to ride. Didn't you?"

Rae stood there turning red. *No, we're friends,* she tried to say, but the words wouldn't come. They weren't friends, were they? Not really. And they'd both made a big mistake.

"What did *you* want?" she asked, in a choking voice—because it wasn't all her. Eden had done at least half of it.

Now Eden turned red, and angry tears filled her eyes. She stormed away toward the tack room. Rae was left standing there. In the aisle of a stable. Where she should have been perfectly happy.

No one was around. She slipped into Guillaume's stall. The dark pony tipped an ear toward her and went on chewing his hay. He had never loved her back, except sometimes when she had an apple in her hand. And that was okay. He was a pony; he had a right to his opinions. But it was easier than Rae had expected to say goodbye and walk out of the barn.

Eden's mother was waiting in the car. "You girls are quiet tonight," she commented on the way home. No one answered.

The minivan stopped in front of her house. Rae slid open the middle door. "Sorry," she whispered near Eden's ear, as she got out. Eden didn't move or speak.

～

Rae waited a couple of days to tell Gammer, who was indignant. "She can't be a very nice child!"

"I wasn't nice either," Rae said. "I was friends with her again because of the riding."

"And then you didn't even get to ride. Well, I guess we've all fooled ourselves that way a time or two!" Gammer said. "And you did learn a lot. You look great out there on Rusty these days. Even I can tell."

"I need real lessons," Rae said. That was the conclusion she'd come to, after a couple of nights trying not to cry about this. A pony, her pony, *here*, was no closer, but she could be learning more, getting ready. "I've got money saved. I think I should go to Tish's riding camp."

"That will take a good chunk of your money," Gammer said. "Still, between us maybe we can manage it without bankrupting you."

But it was too late for this year. Camp was already over.

"Do you want to do individual lessons instead?" Gammer asked.

"No, camp is a better deal," Rae said. "Three whole weeks, and you have the same pony all that time, so it's really concentrated."

"Next year, then," Gammer said. "It's that much more time for us to save our pennies— Oh, I *do* get tired of saying all these wise, encouraging things!" She wrapped her arms around Rae. "Just once I want to let off firecrackers and throw confetti and scream YES at the top of my lungs."

Rae pressed her face into Gammer's apron. She wanted that too, in a distant way. Here and now, she just wanted to cry.

And she was sick of that! Sick of waiting, sick of wanting, sick of hoping and being brave. Sick of making no progress.

"Teach me to bake," she said, pulling back from Gammer's hug. "Really bake. Not pies—something I can do by myself. I want to earn more money."

Gammer put her head on one side, listening past the words to what Rae was really saying. "Money isn't enough to solve this problem. You know that, don't you?"

"It will help," Rae said. "And it will make me feel better to have something to do while I wait!"

"All right," Gammer said. "Money is useful. Don't fall in love with it, though. It's like junk food—tastes good going down, half an hour later you're hungry again."

chapter 20

hungry

PRINCESS had never been left out in the rain for more than fifteen minutes. The only exception was at shows, and when it rained there, the trainer rushed to cover her with a rain sheet.

Out in the field, rain happened. No one cared. It was summer. It was warm. Being wet made Princess itch. She dropped to the ground as the other ponies were doing, and rolled and squirmed in the dirt. She stood up caked with mud. No one rushed to brush it off. Later when the sun came out, drying the mud, that itched too. Princess rolled again and stood up mostly clean, but very rumpled. She shook herself. Dust and grass flew.

As day followed day, her mane grew tangled from wind and rolling and from Skip twining it as he scratched her shoulders. She had mud on her sides and a hairless streak on her flank, where a kick from the oldest mare had peeled off a strip of skin.

Her hooves grew long and the edges chipped off. Luckily it didn't hurt.

She still looked at the house mornings and evenings and wondered. Occasionally the cat appeared, stepping lightly along the top fence rail or hunting in the weeds at the side of the driveway. He rarely came into the pasture. The ponies were inclined to chase him and nip. Princess missed him, but she was in a place where she'd always longed to be, and life was good.

After some hot weeks the air grew cooler, the days shorter. The grass in the field got shorter too, as the trainer had known it would. There were too many ponies. The grass couldn't grow fast enough to feed them all. Someone should have opened the gate to let them into the next field or given them hay. But no human came near the farm, except twice when a small truck drove up the long driveway and a man got out to read the electric meter at the side of the barn. He glanced at the ponies as he drove past the field. That was all.

By now the grass was almost too short for teeth to grasp. There was nothing left to bite off. When Princess tugged at it, it came up by the roots, tasting of dirt and grit. The ground was covered with capsized tufts of grass, their brown roots splayed like the legs of giant spiders. There were areas of gravel, with no grass at all, and those areas were spreading.

The ponies gnawed tree bark. They grubbed continually at the remaining grass. Hunger made them restless and short-tempered. The peaceful moments of standing together, swishing flies and scratching shoulders, became shorter and less peaceful.

Even Princess felt it—anger like an itch in her bones, a

heat in her blood. Whenever she put her head down, some other pony imagined she'd found grass. Ponies lunged at her, punched her with their teeth, kicked her in the sides. They were all so hungry.

The first time Skip bit her, Princess ran. Nothing in her life had trained her to fight back. She'd been her mother's darling, and then she'd lived alone. She was the newest in this herd, so of course she should get out of the others' way.

But the next day she found a dandelion, growing near the back post of the run-in shed. It was tiny and bitter. Still, she grubbed deeper, going for the root, when suddenly she heard hooves behind her. It was Skip. She was trapped.

Anger flared inside her like a lightning flash. She flattened her ears and showed her teeth, lashed her tail and punched out with a hind foot. Skip stopped in his tracks and pricked his ears respectfully. Princess slung her head at him, making an evil face, and finished her dandelion root.

Skip never bit her again. A few others learned to back off as well. But the herd was dominated by fierce old mares who were not to be trifled with. A younger pony on the rise was a threat to be put down. They intensified their attacks. Princess was always on guard now, always watching.

It wore on her. All the ponies grew thin, but Princess was the thinnest. Her ribs showed, even through her shaggy autumn coat. Life was simpler if she kept to herself. She had limited strength. She must save it for finding food.

By now the trees at the bottom of the field had been stripped of bark as high up as the tallest pony could reach. The ponies scalped moss from the rocks, a bitter, meager food. As tree roots worked up through the trampled ground, they were gnawed off.

Still no one came. Once the cat brought a dead mouse, dangling by its tail, and dropped it in front of Princess. She nosed the little corpse. It was soft and smelled of blood. Edible. The cat ate them, after all—

Another pony, a tough old mare, charged. Princess dodged, the mare put her head down, and there was a horrible crunching. The cat trotted away, flicking his tail indignantly.

The days got colder. The long, frosty nights sparkled with stars. The cat sometimes huddled on Princess's back to warm his toes. Deep in her bones, she felt winter coming.

Winter had never mattered before. She'd been indoors, with her blanket on, with hay and grain delivered twice a day.

Now she was outdoors, with no shelter, with nothing to eat. There was long grass outside the fence, but she couldn't reach it, not even down on her knees. She couldn't break the fence, either. It was strong and in good repair. The old man had always seen to that.

Sometimes Princess looked up at the house. In this hungry place she remembered brown sugar. She remembered him.

muffins

RAE became a muffin-maker. "Muffins are easy, and they sell," Gammer told her. "And you can put anything in a muffin! Choose something that lets you be creative, if you plan to be in it for the long haul."

Rae started with blueberry muffins, since she and Gammer were already picking blueberries for pies. She paid for her berries with some of her pony money. "I'll loan you flour and sugar and so forth, to get started," Gammer said, "and the hens are laying, so there's your eggs."

"You can use our muffin tins," Dad said, "as long as I get a muffin for breakfast once in a while."

Blueberry muffins were easy, and when Rae had a whole tray of them lined up on the kitchen counter, she felt better than she had in months. They sold well, but blueberry-cornmeal muffins sold even better. When berry picking ended, Rae wanted to buy frozen berries. Gammer advised against it.

"Cook with the seasons. Your fruit will be cheaper and it will be what people have a hankering for."

So Rae moved on to apple muffins—apple-cinnamon, apple-cheddar. Those were the ones that got Sam and Tully making muffins too. "We have two camps to pay for in our family," Tully said.

"And you sell out so fast, it's obvious there's a market," Sam added.

They branched out into Saturday bake sales on the sidewalk near Sam and Tully's apartment. Gammer helped them develop a pumpkin muffin recipe—a bit dull until Rae realized what it needed was the tang of dried cranberries.

"What charity is this for?" customers sometimes asked.

"We're raising money for camp," Rae always said, but she started to wonder. *Should* they be raising money for charity? Was it wrong to do this for themselves?

"If we can't take care of ourselves, we'll *be* a charity," Sam said, when Rae brought it up.

"We could put out a donation jar, though," Tully said. "People could put their change in. What charity?"

"The animal shelter," Rae said. And with a photo of a kitten to draw people's eyes, the donation jar soon attracted almost everyone's change.

October brought frosty mornings and more customers. Some bought muffins by the dozen. Sam and Tully made hot mulled cider and the spicy scent drew people down the sidewalk.

"I'm not doing this after Thanksgiving, though," Tully said, jumping up and down to keep warm.

"Me either. Writers need their fingers," Sam said, blowing on hers. "We can start up again in the spring."

chapter 22

wild
meat

PRINCESS had gone out on autumn mornings in her old life, when the grass was white and brittle. But she'd never been out all night as the temperature dropped and the air began to bite. Never tried to eat the last meager tips of frozen grass. Never felt how cold sapped the heart out of you and melted off the last bit of fat.

The field was brown now. The white fence rails looked brown too, where the ponies had gnawed them, gazing at the next field. There the grasses were dark green, so heavy they had fallen over with their own weight.

But the fence was strong, and worst of all, it was high, as befitted a fence to keep in Connemaras. All the ponies could do was gaze, while their hunger sharpened.

~

Miles away, a woman with bandages on her face stepped out of a small roadside motel room, phone in hand. She made a call, glancing back at the room. A man with a trustworthy blond mustache sat watching television. The mustache and other alterations made him look younger than the woman; that would change when she recovered from her surgery.

She lifted the phone to her ear, walking to the far side of the parking lot, and spoke in a warm, reassuring voice. "It's Darlene, Charlie's wife. Just letting you know everything's fine here at the farm. No need to worry about a thing!"

She rang another number and spoke in a very different tone of voice. "About that herd of ponies—let's give it a week or two more. I understand zoos pay more when the meat is extra-lean for the tigers—"

"Darlene?" the man called from inside.

"I'll be in touch," the woman said calmly. She turned the phone off and walked back inside.

PRINCESS was warming herself in the sun's pale rays on a cold November afternoon when a car whooshed up the farm driveway, followed by a truck pulling a long, battered trailer. Both stopped near the fence. The ponies galloped toward them in a hungry stampede. Princess followed at the back of the herd, the best place to stay out of trouble.

The car door opened and a woman got out, a small woman in a broad-brimmed hat and sunglasses. Her face was swathed in a green chiffon scarf. Two men climbed down from the truck and looked at the ponies.

"They're lean, all right," the driver said.

"Lean enough?" the woman asked.

"Oh yeah—and they'll be leaner before they get to Canada. No food or water on the road—that's what does it. By the time they hit the meat market they look like antelopes."

"Funny," the other man said, not as if he cared much. "If we're hauling cattle for people to eat, we're supposed to keep 'em fat and not stressed. But to feed big cats they want 'em stressed and skinny, like wild meat."

The woman tapped her foot on the gravel. "Let's get moving, shall we?" She opened the gate and the driver backed the trailer through it, filling the space completely. Then the woman opened the trailer door and disappeared inside. She came out with a lead rope and a bucket. Every eye in the herd locked onto it. She shook it, and it rattled.

Oats. There were oats in there. Princess knew that dry slither. She knew that smell.

The other ponies crowded forward, jostling and nipping. Princess hung back. She didn't want to get kicked. Besides, the woman seemed familiar. She flared her nostrils, testing the air. Sweat and cigarettes—those were the scents of the two men. The woman's scent was masked with medication and perfume and a rank odor rolling out of the truck.

Other ponies were starting to notice it too, but hunger drove them. The old mares maneuvered Skip toward the front. If there was danger, it was his role as the youngest male to discover it.

But Skip wasn't anticipating danger. He was thinking only of food. He stretched his quivering nose toward the oats. As he snatched a mouthful, the woman snapped the rope onto his halter. "Got you!"

Princess knew that voice, knew it well.

The breeze shifted, and a dark stench belched from the trailer, of manure, of despair. Something had happened in there, something dreadful. Animals had suffered for hours, died, been trampled—

The woman led Skip toward the trailer door, rattling the oats in the pail. The other ponies followed, jostling, pricking their ears. Princess whinnied after them. *Don't go!*

The woman's head turned her way. The shiny black lenses of the sunglasses looked like the eyes of a bug. "Not looking very princess-like, are you, my pretty?"

Princess trotted in a circle, tail flagged high over her back. She neighed again, and a few ponies turned their ears her way. But they were mesmerized by the bucket. They followed as the trainer's wife led Skip toward the trailer door. He was nearly inside now.

Princess's muscles bunched into a furious gallop. She tore around the field, mane and tail and frantic neigh streaming out behind her. *Stop! Stop!* The ponies ignored her. She was a newcomer. They had no reason to trust her judgment. The herd surged behind Skip, as, nose in the bucket, he put one front hoof on the ramp—

"Hey! Get out of there!"

It was the driver. The cat streaked toward a fence post and swarmed to the top of it, as Skip shied violently back. The woman kept a firm grip, but the rope stretched long between them.

This was her chance! Princess galloped straight through the gap between the woman's hands and Skip's head. The rope burned across her chest and flew free. Skip lurched backward, and the woman let out a sharp cry.

Then all the ponies were streaming after Princess, their hooves like thunder. Skip followed, the rope flying behind. Their own running threw fear into the herd, and finally the smell from within the trailer penetrated, the smell of terror, suffering, death. They vanished with Princess, among the ragged woods at the bottom of their field.

The woman stood staring at the palms of her hands, which ran with blood. The men gathered around her. "That stinkin' cat was in the truck stealing my sandwich!" the driver said. He reached down for a rock to throw. The cat leaped from his fence post, shot across the driveway, and vanished into the weeds.

The ponies clustered in the woods and watched as the woman turned on the men angrily, holding up her bloody hands. The driver, acting afraid to touch her, took the scarf from around her face. He attempted to tear it. Finally he fished a jackknife out of his pocket and made a cut in the fabric. The ponies could hear it rip all the way down in the trees where they stood blowing, stamping, watching. She wrapped the two halves of the scarf around her palms. They consulted briefly. The men shrugged, closed the trailer doors, and climbed into the truck. It pulled out of the gateway, roared up to the barn, swooped around the circular driveway, and rattled away downhill.

The gate stood open. Beyond, the hillside was chest-deep in grass. For months the ponies had been gazing at it, smelling it, hearing it rustle. Now the open gate drew them. They stepped out from under the trees. The oldest, boldest mare broke into a trot.

The woman looked up from her hands and saw them coming. For a moment she stared at the skinny herd, and at Princess, thinnest of all, in the back.

"This is the second time you've hurt me," she said. "And the last." She wrapped her arms through the bars of the gate, and with a gasp of pain, swung it shut. The latch clicked. Cursing her hands, the trainer's wife got into her car, and veering slightly from side to side, drove away.

The hillside went still. The houses were empty, the barn was empty, the long driveway was empty, the wide sky was empty. There was no help anywhere.

~

Later that day, Skip's trailing rope caught under a root and trapped him, far from water. He might have died there, but hunger saved him. He gnawed the root, just for something to eat, and eventually the rope came loose.

That night the rope burn across Princess's chest itched and prickled and began to ooze. Two days later, she suddenly felt hot all over. Her bones ached, and she could only move slowly, in short steps. Everything seemed distant, and though she was hot, she shivered. She wasn't even hungry anymore.

In the afternoon, a steady cold rain began. It lasted through the night. Princess stood with head bowed, in deeper and deeper misery, while water rolled off her back and dripped from her belly. The drips felt hot at first, then tepid, then cold.

Sometime near dawn she raised her head and shook herself. She felt chilled, down to her blood, down to her bones. The wound burned fiercely, hurting her with every step. Weak but

113

hungry, she wandered up the hill alone, searching, not finding. She came to the fence and dropped to her knees, reaching under the bottom rail, stretching her neck and lips toward grass.

They'd all done this before, many times. The grass within reach had been nipped off at the roots. But just beyond reach, a large clump had gone limp with frost, and a few strands had toppled toward the field. Princess strained against the bottom rail and managed to catch them in her lips, listening for hoofbeats behind her, as the other ponies rushed to claim her prize.

What she heard instead were voices.

chapter 23

hi, pony

PRINCESS ducked from under the fence rail and scrambled to her feet, staring down the driveway. Two bobbing helmets appeared, then shoulders, then riders—two teenaged boys on bicycles laboring up the hill. They had barely enough breath to speak. "Out of . . . shape much, Bill?" panted the one who was slightly ahead.

"I'm not . . . breakin' a sweat yet." Bill, the second one, stood on his pedals and pumped harder, coming up alongside. "Hi, pony," Bill puffed. "'Bye, pony."

Princess stared at his hunched back and flashing legs. *No! Stop!* She trotted along the fence till she was ahead of the bikers. As they passed once more, she blasted out a snort. They paid no attention.

Princess had never asked a human being for anything in all her life. She'd never had to. All her needs except the deepest ones had been understood and met before the lack was even felt. But these boys were going away. They mustn't. She lifted her head and sent a quavering whinny after them.

"*Woof!*" Bill stopped pedaling and dropped his bike in the ditch. He landed beside it on the ground. "Hey, Corey . . . wait up! This pony wants . . . to talk with me." After a moment he dragged himself to his feet and came to the fence, reached out a friendly hand to Princess, and looked her over. "Wow, you're an old-timer!"

Princess licked his sweaty palm. The ponies' salt block had been devoured months ago, and Bill's hand tasted good.

Corey dropped his bike too and came back, breathing deeply. "Right, the pony wanted to talk!" He leaned both arms on the fence. "Hey, there's more of them." The rest of the herd had stepped to the edge of the trees to stare uphill. Now they galloped toward the boys and Princess. She moved out of their way, and the ponies reached through the rails, straining toward the boys' hands.

"Kind of a ratty-looking bunch," Corey said.

Bill was staring at the pasture. "These ponies are starving!"

"They are thin," Corey said. "But I don't know anything about ponies."

"Look at the trees!" Bill said. "They've eaten all the bark. There isn't a blade of grass left in this field." He pulled out his phone and started punching with his thumbs.

Corey said, "There's grass all over the place out here. Why don't we just open the gate?"

"I'm not sure that's—hi, Aunt Tish?"

Corey turned to the overgrown grass at the side of the road, tearing it up in handfuls. The aroma was overpowering. The ponies whinnied and trampled, and Bill pressed one hand to his ear. "About fifteen—they're so skinny! I can see all their ribs."

He listened for a moment. "Yeah, that place you took me last summer that was having the auction . . . Okay, and it's a bad idea to let them out, right? 'Cause there's grass all over the place, outside the fence . . . okay, we'll do that. See you soon."

He turned to Corey. "She's on her way, and we can't let them out. They'd eat too much, and that could kill them. But we can pick." He dropped to his knees, ripping at the tall grass.

When he and Corey had their arms full, they rushed to the fence and tried to toss the grass over. A dozen eager muzzles intercepted their hands. The strongest, bossiest mares got mouthfuls. The rest got nothing but kicks. The green grass smell and the sound of chewing were a torment to Princess. But there was such turmoil at the fence, such kicking and biting and squealing, she didn't dare go close.

"I hate this!" Bill said, almost crying. "They'll hurt each other! And the old one that whinnied at me hasn't gotten a thing. I'm taking some in to him."

"They'll kill you!" Corey said. "They'll trample you in the dirt. They're desperate!"

"You hold a big handful in front of these guys," Bill said, tearing at the grass again. His hands were streaked with welts from the strong stems. "Tease them—I know, it's mean, but just for a second. While they're watching you, I'll go in."

He ducked between the rails and raced toward Princess. She shied away from him, confused. He was big and fast— but he was carrying grass. He dropped a rustling armful of it and backed away. Princess grabbed an enormous mouthful.

So good.

"Watch it!" Corey called. Two ponies near the back of the herd had noticed them. They cantered toward Bill. He bolted for the fence, while the ponies shouldered Princess aside, searching out every last blade.

The cat had been observing from his hiding place in the weeds. Now he came forward to introduce himself, stroked against their legs, and purred loudly. "Nobody's fed him either!" Corey said. He opened his pack and took the ham out of both sandwiches, fed it to the cat, and gave the bread to the ponies.

A few minutes later a pickup roared up the hill, pulling a battered horse trailer. It stopped near the fence, and a gray-haired woman got out. As she looked at the ponies, her mouth thinned to a sharp, angry line. Without a word she opened the trailer. Bill and Corey rushed inside.

They came out with two hay bales each. Tish followed with one. They opened the bales near the fence and began throwing sections of hay over the ponies' backs, scattering them widely across the bare ground. "More piles than ponies," Tish ordered. "That way they won't have to fight."

The ponies fought anyway, at first. They thought they still had to. But soon each one settled down—even Princess, at the far edge of the herd. The hay was fragrant with summer sun, with herbs and flowers and sweet, sweet grass. No one came to take it from her. Across the pasture, all movement had stopped. The grinding of teeth on hay stems filled the air.

After a while a siren screamed up the hill. The county sheriff had arrived, and a few minutes later a woman came from the animal shelter. They talked to each other. They talked on their phones.

"So the owner had a stroke?" the sheriff said.

"That's what I heard," Tish said. "I don't know him. I live a couple of towns over, and these ponies are in a different league than mine. Or they were."

"The trainer and his wife were still living here," said the animal-shelter woman. "They were supposed to be taking care of things."

"I'll go have a look around," the sheriff said. He came back in a few minutes to say, "They took care of things, all right! This place is stripped!" He gazed grimly at the ponies. "There's a story here. Those two gone, one pony with a rope on . . . Someone tried to catch that one, I'll bet, and when he couldn't, he left them all to starve!"

"Who would do that?" Bill asked. "It's the cruelest thing I ever heard of!"

"Maybe we'll find out someday," the sheriff said.

Tish said, "Meanwhile, the real question is what to do about these ponies."

"We'll get a vet up here this afternoon," the animal-shelter woman said. "And we'll figure out how to contact the owner, or whoever is acting for him if he's incapacitated. These guys are thin, but they're alert and energetic. I'm guessing we'll be able to feed them in place."

"What about that one?" Bill asked, pointing to Princess. "He looks pretty bad."

"*She*," Tish said. "That's a mare. But you're right, she does look bad." Tish ducked between the rails and approached Princess, holding out a hand. "May I touch you?"

Very little could have moved Princess from her hay pile. She chewed steadily, while gentle hands pressed against her ribs and probed her knobby backbone. Then Tish bent to look at the wound on Princess's chest.

"Okay, you need a vet right away." She turned to the sheriff. "This pony has an infected wound that needs immediate care. I'd like to take her home with me."

"Normally that would be a problem," the sheriff said. "Animals are property. I can't just take them from an owner. But there's no one here to take her *from* and nobody living here to provide medical care. So I'd say go ahead. If that's the wrong answer, we'll sort it out later."

Tish got a rope out of the trailer and clipped it to Princess's halter. "Bring the hay, Bill. I don't want her to have to stop eating even for a second."

Bill gathered the hay in his arms. Princess lifted her head to follow it, and Tish read the nameplate on her halter. "'*Princess*.' In quotation marks, so it's probably a stable name. Maybe you were a princess once, darlin', but that was a long time ago!" She led Princess through the gate to the open trailer. "Ever been in one of these?"

Princess had been riding in trailers since she was a month old. Trailers meant shows. They meant clapping and blue ribbons, an old man's proud voice, brown sugar.

Her mane was tangled. Her hooves were ragged. She was skinny and scarred, muddy and cold. But she lifted her head and walked proudly up the ramp.

Bill opened the front door and climbed into the front compartment. "I'll ride in here and hold the hay for her. Corey, throw the bikes in the truck. You can ride up front with Aunt Tish."

"What about him?" Corey asked. The cat was exploring the empty half of the trailer, which smelled appealingly of mouse.

"Bring him along," Tish said. "I can always use another barn cat."

a refuge

PRINCESS braced against the jolts, and never stopped eating. It didn't seem real, to chew a whole mouthful of food and swallow it, and still have some left, to take another bite, and another.

After some time, the trailer stopped. Princess heard barking. Then the ramp was let down, and Tish backed Princess out. The cat streaked past her, arched his body at an elderly, astonished dog, and vanished into the weeds.

Princess saw an old barn and a riding ring with slumping fence rails. Horses and ponies stood out in a field, bright-colored in their blankets. They stared at Princess, and the smallest pony whinnied.

Princess didn't whinny back. She'd had enough of fields and ponies. She tugged on the halter, pulling Tish toward the barn door. "You know your own mind!" Tish said. "Maybe you *are* a princess. Bill, put shavings in the last stall, will you?"

Princess clip-clopped down the barn aisle between rows of stall doors rubbed smooth by horses' necks. She smelled hay, a vast mountain of it somewhere overhead. She smelled grain, liniment, saddle leather, horses, the scents laid down in layers over many years.

Bill appeared with a bale of shavings. Princess followed the river of fresh pine scent into a small, dark stall. Bill dumped the shavings, and Tish took off Princess's halter.

Princess shook herself all over. She'd worn that halter for months. It had made chafe marks on her face and a sore place behind her ears. How good it felt to wear nothing at all!

Tish brought a bucket of warm water. Bill brought more hay. "Hay is the safest food for her," Tish said. "Filling, but not too rich. The vet's on his way. You boys can go if you like."

"I'll stay," Bill said. "I want to hear what he says."

This vet wasn't the one who'd known Princess as a foal. The older man had more or less retired and was even now on his way to his winter home in Florida. This vet was young, efficient, and angry.

He listened to Princess's heart, took her pulse and temperature, and cleaned the wound on her chest. "I'll give her antibiotics, but that's going to leave a scar. Could you hold her, please?" He gave Princess one shot, then another. She stood perfectly still, as she had been taught.

"Well-trained?" Tish said. "Or too sick to struggle?"

"If she were a horse, she'd be dead," the vet said. "But ponies are tough—and this is a young animal." He lifted Princess's upper lip and looked at her teeth. "Only three years old!"

"She looks thirty," Tish said.

"I know. Better blanket her. She doesn't have any fat to keep her warm. Antibiotics twice a day, rub ointment on that wound, and call me if something doesn't seem right. Being young is in her favor. I think we'll pull her through."

The short afternoon was already darkening when he left. Tish brought a blanket, old and patched. The dog had been sleeping on it, Princess could smell, and the front buckles were missing. Tish tied it shut with baling twine. "This sure isn't fit for a princess, but it's warm."

"She will make it, won't she?" Bill asked. "I mean—she won't die?"

"She's in pretty tough shape," Tish answered. "But she's eating . . . oh dear, now she's *not* eating!"

Princess actually couldn't eat, not even one more bite. Her bones were still hungry, but her stomach was full. For the first time in weeks, she wasn't cold. The November wind didn't reach inside the barn. No other pony could threaten her. She was safe.

Her front legs folded. She lowered herself down onto the shavings and closed her eyes.

"All right, that makes me want to cry," Bill said.

~

Later Princess woke to the thud of horses and ponies being led into the barn, feed tubs rattling, water gurgling into pails—all the sounds of a stable at mealtime. Tish brought a pan of warm mash, sweet and grainy-smelling. There was medicine in it, but that didn't spoil the taste. Princess licked the pan clean.

"Good girl!" Tish put down another flake of hay. "You're looking a little perkier, I think. Sleep well, Princess."

She turned out the lights. Princess munched. Owls hooted in the loft, and mice squeaked. Princess listened past the sounds for a certain footstep, a certain wheezy breathing. She was in a barn again. Perhaps it was possible.

Someone finally did appear—the cat, leaping silently to the top of the stall door. He was feeling well-fed, too, and his breath smelled of mouse. He hopped lightly onto Princess's blanketed back and gave a purr. Then he curled up, lulled by the gentle crunch of hay.

chapter 25

tithing

"RAE?" Dad called. "Sam and Tully are on the phone."

They'd seen each other just a couple of hours ago at school, made baking plans for later in the week, picked books to read and science experiments to do after homework. So why would Sam and Tully be calling?

Rae picked up the phone and both voices tumbled out, tangling together.

"—abandoned ponies!"

"—the newspaper—"

"Starving!"

"—the place we went last summer—"

Eventually they slowed down enough to take turns, and Rae heard the whole story. Two boys out biking had discovered a herd of ponies starving in a field at Highover Farm. "The owner's sick or something like that," Sam said. "There was a trainer who was supposed to be taking care of everything—"

"And instead he *took* everything—" Tully said.

"And then he took off," Sam finished.

Rae's stomach lurched. "Will they die?"

"The paper didn't say," Tully said. "That's probably a good sign. The animal shelter's taking care of them right now—"

"Can we help them?" Rae asked.

"They might not need help."

"The owner's still alive—"

Rae left the phone on the table, with their voices coming out of it. She went upstairs and got out her bank statement. She had nearly enough muffin money to pay her share of camp. That was on top of the small fund with which she would someday purchase a not-very-expensive pony. But it was just sitting there, numbers on a piece of paper, when it could be helping.

She swallowed the cherry-pit lump in her throat and went to the window. The small patch of grass beside the barn was brown and weedy from not being grazed. Without even trying, her mind painted them out there, gaunt ponies staring at her with large, haunted eyes.

You can have it, she told them. *You can have it all.*

~

After supper she called Gammer on the computer and told her about the ponies.

"Such a high, lonely place," Gammer said. "I can see how no one would have known what was happening up there. Thank goodness for those boys!"

"How do I write a check?" Rae asked. She'd put everything she earned into the bank. How to get it out again was a mystery.

Gammer pinched the bridge of her nose. "Of course you want to write a check," she said, after a moment. "You're Rae. Since it's a joint account, and you're a minor, you need me to cosign. I can do that from down here, somehow or other, but I'll need to find out how. I'll talk with you tomorrow, okay?"

The next morning Rae woke extra early with an acid feeling in her stomach. She went down to the kitchen, where Dad was making breakfast and packing his lunch. The radio was on, and suddenly Rae heard the word *ponies*.

"—abandoned at Highover Farm. Pleasant Valley Animal Shelter is currently feeding and caring for the ponies. The owner, Roland McDermott, is in a medical facility recovering from a stroke he suffered during the summer, and was unavailable for comment. A spokesperson for the family expressed shock at the abandonment. 'The trainer's wife, Darlene Baker, maintained regular contact with Mr. McDermott's niece and provided assurances that the ponies were being cared for. We are working with the animal shelter and will provide all funds needed for the ponies' continued care.' Details of the abandonment are being kept from Mr. McDermott, lest it cause a health setback. Police are searching for the trainer, Charles Baker, and his wife, Darlene, but they are believed to have left the area."

Dad reached out and pulled Rae into a hug. "You hate this, I bet. But they'll be okay, Rae. Nobody's talking about them dying."

The phone rang after a minute. It was Gammer. "Did you hear the report on the radio?" she asked. She streamed the local station on her computer every morning to keep up with news from home.

"We heard," Rae said.

"They have an owner," Gammer said. "There's money to care for them. So there's no need for you to write a check. You've worked so hard with your muffin-making. I want you to benefit from that."

"But—" Rae said. "But I *want* to help."

Gammer was quiet for a moment. "I'm pulling up your bank statement on my computer. Hmm. You were planning to pay one-third of the camp price, and you have a little ways to go on that—but there's time. If you really want to, Rae, you could tithe. That means setting aside a certain percent of your profits for giving away. I've been doing that for years."

"Who do you give it to?" Rae asked.

"I have a favorite charity," Gammer said with a smile in her voice. "Now, you're a young person running your first business. I'd say give two percent—of your *profits*, not your gross."

Rae knew the difference. Gross sales meant all the money you took in. Profit was what remained after you took out your expenses.

"It won't seem like much at first," Gammer said, "but over time, if you tithe regularly, it will add up. Like your savings did. So if you want, I'll make an estimate of what two percent would be, and write a check to the shelter. Does that help you feel better?"

It did, and strangely, that made Rae start crying. "Oh Gammer, shut inside that huge fence, they must have been so *hungry!*"

chapter 26

new world

"PRINCESS, here's your mash."

"Would you like more hay?"

"Drink your water while it's warm."

"How are you feeling?"

That was Princess's new world. All of it. Twice a day Tish peeled back the blanket, sucked in her breath, and dabbed ointment on the wound. It hurt, in a distant way. Everything seemed distant, hardly worth paying attention to. Would she be here long? Maybe not. Maybe she was going somewhere else soon.

After several days the pain sharpened. Princess flinched when the ointment went on. The vet came and seemed pleased. "That's looking better, actually. The swelling's gone down so she feels it more, and now she has the energy to react."

He started to put the blanket back on, but Tish said, "No, I want to clean her up first. I think she'll feel better if she doesn't look so awful."

She got out a box of brushes and groomed Princess, avoiding the kick and bite marks. "There! That's better. Now let's see about your mane."

That wasn't so easy. Princess's mane hung in dark, matted knots that the comb would barely penetrate. "What a mess! I don't have time for this!" Tish got her clippers and plugged them in. "Is this going to scare you? You don't look like you've ever been clipped in your life!"

She briefly turned on the clippers.. Princess didn't twitch at the familiar sound. "You're being a little *too* good," Tish muttered. "Maybe you're just feeble. I wish you could talk!"

She turned the clippers on again. They buzzed along the top of Princess's neck. *Flup flup flup*—her long, tangled mane dropped in pieces to the floor. Her neck felt light and bare and chilly.

Tish said, "Oh dear. You look totally pathetic! Let's get your blanket back on."

Bill appeared at the end of the aisle. "Did you have to butch all her hair off?"

"I regret it now," Tish said. "But it'll grow back. What are you doing here, anyway? Don't you have football practice?"

"Not today. I came to check on my pony."

"Since when are you into ponies?"

"Is it okay for her to have an apple?" Bill was reaching into his pocket as he spoke. Princess lifted her muzzle to his face, drawing in his scent. It brought back that day—the voices after the long silence, and the kind hands picking grass.

"Hey, what's she doing?" Bill asked. "That tickles!"

"Ponies greet each other by smelling noses," Tish said. "Puff your breath back at her."

Bill puffed. Princess puffed. Then her velvety upper lip twitched on Bill's cheek. "What was that? Did she try to *bite* me?"

"More like a kiss," Tish said. "She knows who saved her life!"

Bill blushed and kissed her soft nose. "Don't tell anybody I did that. I mean—I'm a football player!"

Bill was also a basketball player, a wrestler, a snowboarder. He didn't visit every winter week, but he did drop in often. Once Corey came too. That time Bill didn't kiss Princess, but other times he did.

Princess continued to improve. Once a week, Tish took the blanket off, groomed her lightly, and put a measuring tape around her belly. Every week Princess weighed a little bit more. The wound on her chest stopped hurting and started itching. Her legs began to feel like moving again. She started pacing her stall.

"You need exercise," Tish said. One January morning, she led Princess outdoors. The snow was high and white, the sky a deep brilliant blue. The sun was warm, though, and the air smelled particularly fresh. Princess stared around her, at the unfamiliar house, the paddocks full of horses and ponies.

"Your eyes are sparkling!" Tish said. "You do look somewhat princess-like this morning." She led Princess to a small corral near the barn. Inside was a little red pony and three piles of hay.

"Princess, meet Radish," Tish said. "You two should be friends. Radish gets along with everybody."

Tish took off the halter. Princess went straight to the nearest hay pile. She wasn't interested in friends; she was interested in food.

But before she'd taken three bites, Radish walked toward her, ears pointed forward. At her? At the hay? Princess wasn't sure. She circled to another pile, took a mouthful and put up her head to watch.

Radish came toward her. Princess circled away. Radish followed. How rude! She just wanted to eat in peace. Was that too much to ask? She put her ears back and showed her teeth. Radish kept coming.

Princess turned and kicked. She didn't touch Radish, not even close, but her heels made a vicious swish through the air. Radish stopped, blinking in a friendly way. Maybe he wanted to be friends. But Princess had learned her lesson. Girls and ponies couldn't be trusted. *Stay away!* she told Radish, with her flattened ears and angry face and her back foot ready to kick again.

Tish seemed busy in the barn, but she observed it all. The next day when Princess was led to the paddock, there was one pile of hay, and Radish was on the other side of the fence.

From then on, she ate outdoors in peace, watching the enormous icicles drip in the sun, observing the other horses. Once in a while Radish reached his head over the fence to greet her. She always walked away.

"Why is Princess all by herself?" Bill asked when he visited.

133

"That's how she wants it," Tish said. "She had a rough time out in that field. I think she just doesn't want to be bothered."

That was true. Still, the days were long and empty. Tish was a kind woman, and busy. The cheerful greeting with breakfast, the "goodnight" with supper, the twenty minutes of daily care were pleasant, and Princess was grateful. Still, she remembered when her life was fuller, when someone came every morning with love and brown sugar.

~

Far to the south, under a palm tree, a woman with a new name and altered face applied tangerine-colored polish to her long, curved nails. She looked quite different these days. Her hair was frosty. Her face seemed smoother and younger. The palms of her hands were somewhat pink and tender—the result of a car accident, she'd told her husband, and there had been an accident. She'd lost control of her car that cold afternoon, driving back to the airport.

The trainer came out of their condo, carrying a breakfast tray and trailed by a fat corgi. The corgi was half-blind and located his new owner mainly by the smell of toasted English muffin wafting from the tray. The dog couldn't have known how different the trainer looked, with his short pale hair and trustable bristling mustache.

"Crumpet, my dear?" he asked in a clipped voice, setting the tray on the low table.

"Best not call them crumpets, darling," the wife said, in the same kind of voice. "They aren't crumpets, and *real* English people know that."

The trainer sighed and dropped into the other chair, lapsing into his normal accent. "You know, I miss the ponies."

"The money's still rolling in. I sold one of his vases the other day for a good price."

"You're being careful, right? We don't want anything traced."

"I'm being quite, quite careful."

chapter 27

dragon faces

"PRINCESS, you're getting plump!" the vet said, when he came to do spring shots. "Too much time on pasture."

Tish said, "I want to make it up to her for what she's been through."

"I understand," the vet said, "but her body has adapted to survive on very little. Spring grass is too rich. Cut her grazing to a couple of hours a day, and use her in your riding program. She needs exercise."

"I don't even know if she's saddle-trained," Tish said. "But if she were mine, I'd find out!"

"I'm sure you could get permission," the vet said. "The owner's niece is way over her head with the ponies. She's eager to do the right thing, but she has no idea what that is."

"I guess it's worth exploring," Tish said. That evening she

telephoned the old man's niece, Ms. Calloway, and explained what the vet recommended.

"I haven't even told Uncle what happened with the ponies," Ms. Calloway said. "He'll be so upset. I want to wait until he's stronger. So I guess it's up to me, isn't it?"

"I guess it is," Tish said.

"Would you need more money for her care, if you start using her? I'm happy to send more."

"No, if anything I should be paying you," Tish said.

"Oh no no no! I want to do what's right for the pony, and I want to pay for the poor creature's care. I know Uncle would."

"Then I'd like to try it," Tish said. "But call Dr. Janysyn and make sure you understand why he's recommending it."

"I'll do that," Ms. Calloway said. "I know how important it is to be careful. I feel as if I should have known, somehow, that that woman was lying . . ."

"Honest people blame themselves," Tish said. "The other kind blame everyone else. You had no way of knowing—and you were deceived by someone who was good at it."

"Oh, thank you!" Ms. Calloway said. "She was good at it. I'll try to remember that. And I will check with the vet. Thank you, Tish. You've relieved my mind considerably." She called back the next morning, and the answer was yes.

Princess missed the long hours on pasture, hours in which she never stopped gulping down grass even for a second. She ate as much as she could in the two hours she was allowed to graze, and of course there was hay. Warm weather and the change of diet made her feel alive, energetic, eager for something.

One morning Tish and Judy, the young woman who'd been coming to help her, got Princess out of her stall, groomed her, put on a saddle and bridle, and led her to the ring—a much bigger ring than the one at Highover, with a row of jumps set up in the middle to divide it in half.

"Let's see if she's ever been lunged." Tish attached a long line to Princess's bridle. She had a whip with her, with a trailing lash. Princess caught the moment when the whip lifted. She knew what that meant. Calmly she began walking in a circle around Tish, out at the end of the line.

"Hmm!" Tish said. She asked for a trot, a whoa, another trot, a canter. She had Princess switch directions and repeat it all.

"Okay! She knows more about lunging than I do! Let's try her under saddle."

At the mounting block, Princess stood perfectly still while Tish got on. She was heavier than any of Princess's girls, but she settled into the saddle in a skillful way that made her feel light. With a touch of her heels, she asked Princess to walk.

Princess stepped forward, listening with her whole body. All Tish's kindness and knowledge came through in the way she used her hands and legs. She asked softly for each bend and turn and speed change, and Princess answered just as softly.

"Wow!" Judy said. "She's perfect!"

"Almost too perfect," Tish agreed. "I like school ponies with a bit of an edge to them, so the kids get challenged. I wonder if she's ever jumped."

"Try her!" Judy said. "All the jumps are right there."

"All right, lower that rail in the center. I want this to be easy for her."

Judy put the rail down to about knee height, and Tish pointed Princess at it.

Princess hesitated. What did Tish want? It was a fence. She should stop, right? Nobody had ever ridden her toward a fence and expected her to jump it. But Tish's hands on the reins kept her straight, and Tish's legs and intention said, *Over*.

Over, then! The rail wasn't much higher than the log in the field, but with Tish on her back it would be harder. Princess gathered herself and exploded in an enormous bound, clearing the rail with two feet to spare.

Judy clapped and hooted, and Tish burst out laughing. She brought Princess to a standstill. "Good girl! Okay, Judy, go saddle Banner, and let's see how she handles another horse in the ring. She's a bit of a loner, our Princess, but hopefully she can cope."

A few minutes later Judy rode into the ring on a tall, black, spirited-looking horse. Princess had seen him from a distance, and that seemed like a good way to see him. He looked fast. If he wanted to bite her, she wouldn't be able to get away.

Tish trotted Princess around the ring. Judy trotted Banner. His strides were long, and soon Princess saw him coming up behind her, too tall, too near. As he came alongside, she flattened her ears and swung her head around, showing her front teeth. *Watch it!*

"Princess!" Tish said sharply. "No!"

They circled the ring again. Again Banner passed. Again

Princess swung her head, despite Tish's warning. She couldn't help it. Her rump remembered being bitten. Her sides remembered being kicked. *Back off!* she told Banner. *Stay away!* She did everything else Tish asked, but she couldn't stop giving Banner warnings, and Tish's voice grew more and more unhappy.

Finally she stopped Princess in the middle of the ring. Judy brought Banner in, close enough so they could talk.

"I can't use her," Tish said. "Not if she's going to make dragon faces at every pony that passes."

"But she didn't kick," Judy said.

"No," Tish admitted. "She didn't kick. She's very well trained—in fact, she's a super pony. But those faces would scare kids into fits!"

"Not every kid," Judy said. "Anyway, a few minutes ago you were worried she was too perfect!"

"You're right," Tish said. "All right, go saddle Nubbin. He's bomb-proof, and you couldn't hurt those legs with a baseball bat! We're going to push her hard. If she's got a kick in her, I want to find out now."

She walked Princess around the ring while they waited. Princess felt Tish's worry. What was the matter, though? The black horse had left, and the rest of the ride had gone beautifully. It was peaceful out here, just the two of them—

"Oh, I hope this works!" Tish murmured. "You are an amazing pony, Princess. But maybe we just got to the bottom of why you were in that field. How could he sell you if you did that in the show ring!"

Judy arrived riding a fat brown pony who moved slowly, sighing each time Judy tapped him with her heels. Princess had seen him before too. He didn't scare her, but that didn't mean she wanted to be near him.

Tish asked Princess to stop. "Okay, Judy, bring Nubbin up behind us, and I mean *right* up. Really crowd her."

Judy rode Nubbin close, closer. "Even closer!" Tish said.

He was touching her! Princess could feel his breath! He lowered his head and actually *shoved* her from behind!

Princess wanted to lash out with both hind feet. She wanted to run. No pony should be this close to her, not even fat old Nubbin. But Tish was here. Judy was here—and if people were around, they were in charge. She had learned that at birth.

Princess flattened her ears until they disappeared in her short mane. She twisted her neck around to make a terrible face at Nubbin. She slashed him with her tail. But she stood still, as Tish asked, and after a moment, Nubbin backed off.

"All right!" Tish said, "Ninety-nine ponies in a hundred would have kicked, and I wouldn't blame them."

"So you'll use her?" Judy said. "Hurray!"

"She'll break hearts," Tish said. "She's exactly the kind of pony kids fall in love with." She dismounted and gave Princess a friendly hug around the neck. "I'm half in love with her myself!"

Princess let the hug happen, though hugs weren't her favorite thing. At this moment Tish felt all bubbly, like the girls who used to ride her and win blue ribbons. Princess turned her head toward the gate, where no one waited.

chapter 28

registered

RAE, Sam, and Tully started making strawberry-rhubarb muffins after Gammer came home from Florida in the spring. The kitchen was always busy and smelled so good Dad said he was gaining weight just from the scent. They baked twice a week now, to sell at the stores where Gammer sold pies. Quickly, the camp funds reached their goals. Rae started to put money into the pony fund. Once a month she and Gammer sent a check to the animal shelter, which started to mail her its special donor newsletter.

Rae checked Tish's website every morning when she woke up, and every lunch period at school, and every evening before she went to bed. She read and reread the camp description:

"Three-week horsemanship camp. A fun, low-key introduction to riding and caring for ponies and horses.

Daily riding classes, culminating with competition at the Annual Pleasant Valley Animal Shelter Benefit Horse Show at Portchester Farm. Each camper will be assigned a horse or pony to care for and ride. Helmets and boots required. Pack your own lunch. Registration opens in late April, first come, first served."

"When exactly *is* late April?" she asked Sam and Tully.

"The last week," Tully said.

"I think it's looser than that," Sam said. "Watch that website like a hunting gecko. Wait, do geckos hunt? Anyway, that 'first come, first served' line? That means it's popular."

"That's right," Tully said. "Like—they could sell out fast. You definitely want to be first served!"

Rae checked even more often after that. On April 27, just before bedtime, she made her last check of the day and discovered the words, highlighted in blue:

"Camp registration open."

"Dad! We can register!"

"Good. We'll get it done first thing in the morning," he said, standing back to squint at a dachshund he was constructing out of an old wrench.

"No, *now!*" Rae said. "It's first come, first served."

"Then it better be now. Do you want help?"

"No," Rae said, clicking the registration form open. She didn't want to waste a second. With Dad watching over her shoulder, she worked her way through the boxes. Name. Address. Experience level. "Beginner?" Dad asked. "Or intermediate? You do know a lot, Rae."

Rae liked the word *intermediate*. After all, she had watched a million of Eden's lessons and practiced them on Rusty. She checked that box.

"Payment method? What should I put?"

"Check," Dad said. "You and Gammer will each write me one, and I'll send the camp the full amount."

So boldly, knowing the money was in the bank, Rae registered.

which?

PRINCESS hated change, ever since the ambulance morning when everything had changed forever. Winter had changed to spring, and to summer. That was acceptable. But here came a new routine. Someone rode her every day—never the same person, never at the same time, each learner asking something different. Back when she was a foal and the days were all the same, she had loved anything new. These days every change made her worry about tomorrow. Right now she had food. Would she always? Right now she had Tish and Judy and sometimes Bill, people who appeared regularly and wished her well. Might that end? Each new rider opened a fresh door to some unknown future.

These weren't thoughts, exactly, more like a gnawing feeling in her belly—a lot like hunger.

It got worse as the stable got busier. Riders wanted to brush up their skills before Mrs. Portchester's annual show, and they had to get their lessons in early. When camp started, all other lessons stopped. Princess was so well-behaved, Tish used her often.

"She's grinding her teeth," Judy reported one day. "Could she have ulcers?"

"I hope not, but anything's possible."

Tish changed the way she fed Princess. Now there was always hay available, in a hay net with very small openings. Princess could only tear out a tiny bite at a time. She was never hungry, but never quite full either, and whatever it was still gnawed at her gut.

Dr. Janysyn came again. "You're doing everything right," he said. "I'm afraid it's stress-related."

"She's a super lesson pony," Tish said. "Never puts a foot wrong. But I guess that takes a toll on her."

"Pull her out of the program," he suggested.

"Unfortunately, camp starts next week, and I've got the same number of campers as I do ponies!"

"Medication, then," the vet said. "She'll feel a lot better, and afterward we'll figure out what comes next. I understand the owner is making gains. Maybe he'll be able to weigh in."

That night Princess's mash tasted odd, and soon after the gnawing in her gut stopped. But with nowhere else to go, worry zinged down her legs and shot along her neck into her brain. For the first time in her life, it was hard to be good. She had to work at it.

Some memories helped. A rich voice saying *"That's* my Princess!" Brown sugar on a trembling palm.

~

RAE spent hours on Rusty after school, with a riding book balanced against his garden-trowel ears. She struggled to sit perfectly, heels aligned with hips aligned with shoulders and ears. Rusty never moved unexpectedly or disobeyed, and Rae was pretty sure, after much study, that the old saddle bolted to his back was not ideal for sitting in a good position. So this wasn't perfect, but it was the preparation she could do.

For which pony? That was the question that had taken over every waking hour, the one Sam and Tully looked forward to escaping when they went off to their own camps. Rae got that, but what else could she think about? For three weeks she'd have a pony of her own. Three whole weeks. Who would it be?

She knew some of Tish's ponies from her three lessons at the stable. When she couldn't sleep at night, she lined them up in her mind and ranked them. Which one did she want most? Radish. Which one did she want least? Nubbin.

Then she'd apologize to Nubbin, who was fat and slow, more like a couch than a pony, but so wise and dear. She'd imagine spending three weeks with him, imagine it in detail. Even that would be the best three weeks ever.

"How are you not going to ruin your life over this?" Sam asked.

"Yeah," Tully said. "How will you not fall in love with this pony and break your heart?"

"I'm going to fall in love with him," Rae said. "Totally. For three weeks. I know ahead of time that it's only for a little while, and then it's over. So why hold back?"

"That might work," Tully said. "Like a camp crush. A lot of people have those."

"But this is Rae," Sam said. "And a pony! You be careful, okay? Stick to the plan."

"Yes," Rae said.

chapter 30

the
big day

"PRINCESS, it's the big day!" That was Judy, bringing breakfast extra early one blue-sky summer morning.

Breakfast was always welcome, but why now and not at the normal time? Princess ate in haste, as much haste as the hay net allowed. All down the barn aisles she heard the sound of energetic munching. Early breakfast meant something to the other horses. They knew what was about to happen. Princess heard that in their snorts and stomps, but *what* did they know?

When they'd finished, Tish and Judy led them to the ring and tied them to posts along one side. Cars began to pull into the driveway, and children got out, more and more of them. Their voices sent the cat racing to the hayloft.

Princess would have liked to go away too, but when she was tied, she wasn't supposed to even fidget. That's what the trainer had taught her. She braced her zinging legs, raised her head, and gazed off into the distance the way she used to at shows, putting most of herself somewhere else.

~

RAE hugged her stomach to hold in the butterflies. She didn't know any of these kids, but that didn't matter. She knew the ponies. Nubbin, Ginger, and Macaroon were the beginner ponies, the ones she'd had lessons on. There were three chestnuts whose names she didn't remember. Then came Radish, Banner, Shoo-fly, Asterix, Cajun, and a new pony down at the end.

Rae had trained herself out of wanting beautiful ponies like that one—a stunning dapple-gray mare with legs as black and beautifully shaped as wrought iron, large dark eyes, and a mane and tail drawn on with a number two pencil. She was sturdy and rounded, yet elegant, and the perfect size, big enough for an adult, small enough not to be intimidating to a kid. It took Rae a moment to notice the red ribbon braided into her tail. A bad sign, and she didn't seem at all friendly, staring off into the distance like that. She had a scar on her chest, too, visible all the way across the ring. There must be a story behind that.

Radish, meanwhile, stood looking cheerful and innocent, as his busy mouth worked at untying his rope. Rae's insides melted like marshmallow. He perfectly filled the pony-shaped hole in her heart.

Would she get him? Probably not. Radish had a reputation. Even the few times Rae had come here, she'd heard stories. He would go to a very experienced rider. Still, she wasn't a beginner. It was possible . . .

Tish raised her hand for quiet. "Hello, campers! And welcome. For the next three weeks you'll learn how to care for and ride horses and ponies. You'll each have an assigned mount, and you're going to meet that animal right now."

Voices clamored. "I want the black horse!" "I want the cute one!" "I want that pretty one down at the end!"

Tish held up her hand again. When silence fell, she went on. "I've paired you off based on how much you know about riding, and how much I know about these animals."

Radish Radish Radish, Rae thought, crossing her fingers. Then she noticed Nubbin, standing there half-asleep, and her heart twisted. Nubbin would be *fine*.

"However, my choice isn't cast in stone," Tish went on. "If the chemistry isn't right, I'll switch you around. Bear in mind that I may not be able to find a perfect fit. But that's part of what I teach—how to ride any pony, not just your dream pony."

Dream pony. An image flashed through Rae's mind—that black foal, years ago at the show. Who knew where she was now, or even what she looked like? Maybe she'd grown up to be nothing special—though that seemed unlikely.

But right now, Radish was her dream pony.

"Steve," Tish said. "You'll work with Nubbin."

Oh good, Rae admitted to herself. *But I love you, Nubbin.*

"Lori, you'll have Banner."

Also good. Banner was tall and elegant, but definitely not a pony.

"Rae, I'm putting you on Radish," Tish said.

Rae gasped aloud. Had she heard that right? Tish chuckled. "I'm glad you're pleased. Amber? You'll ride Princess—that's her down at the end."

⁓

PRINCESS reluctantly turned her head as Amber approached. "Yay, I got the pretty one!" she whispered, giving Princess an admiring stroke on the nose.

Princess held herself motionless. Pats on the nose were not her favorite thing. The girl seemed excited, like the girls who'd ridden her at shows. But was this a show? It didn't seem like one.

"Before you start grooming your ponies," Tish said, "let me draw everyone's attention to Princess. See the red ribbon in her tail? Who can tell me what that means?"

The dark-haired girl with Radish raised her hand. "She kicks?"

"Yes, Rae, that's right. Princess was found starving in a field with a herd of other ponies, and it looks like she got pushed around by them. She doesn't kick, but if you ride up close behind her, she'll make a dragon face. Let the red ribbon be a reminder to stay out of her space."

Now everyone was looking at Princess. She was used to admiring crowds, but this felt different. Uncomfortable. She turned her head away, looking off at the distant trees.

Tish handed out grooming kits and explained all the brushes. Amber already knew how to use them, and she gave Princess a thorough cleaning. Princess held perfectly still, but inside she flinched as new hands did new things—none of them disrespectful, none of them wrong, but different from the way Tish had been doing them for the past few months.

Tish explained how to pick up a horse's hoof and clean it. Then she and Judy went down the line, making sure that every camper could do the job safely. It was all perfectly calm. Princess wasn't. Riding lessons she understood, though she didn't love them. But this wasn't a riding lesson.

Next came leading. Princess had never encountered anyone who didn't know how to do that, but apparently some people didn't.

Amber did know. Right hand holding the rope close under Princess's jaw, left hand holding the excess rope, folded, not coiled, and staying level with Princess's shoulder, she marched them over to Banner and Lori. "Isn't she *gorgeous*? I never dreamed I'd get to ride a Highover pony!"

Lori looked back over her shoulder, as Banner towed her along. "I know—and Princess is the perfect name for her. Hey, dude, slow down!" She turned him in a circle that brought him close to Princess.

Too close. Princess's legs were zinging with nervous energy. It was all she could do not to run or kick. Instead she slung her head at Banner, ears fiercely back, jaws open wide. *Back off!*

Amber let out a shriek. Lori yelled, "Whoa!"

"You guys okay?" Tish called. "Lori, remember the red ribbon. Give Princess space."

Lori led Banner away to the other side of the ring. Princess felt good about that. But Amber had gone all stiff and quiet. She kept casting sideways glances at Princess, biting her lips. Afraid? No human had ever feared Princess. It felt terrible. People were supposed to be in charge. They were supposed to think of everything, and know what to do, and do it. Amber wasn't like that, and Tish, who was, was way off at the other end of the ring.

~

RAE knew how to lead ponies from reading and from handling Guillaume. She paid close attention to Tish anyway, trying to walk exactly parallel to Radish's head, trying not to melt as his small muzzle quivered. She loved his short, bouncy steps, his extra-aliveness. If he were only a couple of hands taller, she would be seriously, permanently in love. In spite of the nips he kept aiming at her thighs when he thought she wasn't looking. In spite of the mischievous look in his eyes—

"Rae? Did you hear me? We're going in for lunch!"

Already? Rae had spent half a day with Radish already? There were only going to be sixteen of them—three weeks of five days each, plus the Saturday of the show. So only fifteen and a half days left.

"Ponies eat before people," Tish said, back at the barn. She demonstrated how to fill a hay net, and tie it high and tight so a pony couldn't catch his foot in it, then sent all the campers off to do it. Rae stuffed and hung a net for Radish. Then she got her lunch bag and headed back to his stall.

"Rae, we'll eat at the picnic table," Tish said.

"I'll eat with Radish," Rae said.

Tish smiled and shook her head. "I was taught to leave ponies alone while they're eating—and that's what I teach here. Besides, you want to get to know people, right?"

Not really. Rae had forty-nine other weeks in the year to get to know people, only three to get to know Radish. She sat next to Amber, who didn't talk much, and shared turkey out of her sandwich with a tough-looking cat. This was a little like school without Sam and Tully, or even Eden. But she was here! She'd made it. She was going to ride Radish for three whole weeks. She touched the hoof-pick belt buckle, which Dad had made for Mom as an engagement present. *Thank you, Mom.* Because without that spine of steel she wouldn't be here.

And *thank you, Gammer,* because she had a strawberry-rhubarb hand pie in her lunchbox, big enough to share with Amber, which made it easier to talk.

"Okay, time to saddle up," Tish said at last.

Rae raced to the barn, slowing to a walk beside the sign that said *No Running, Please.* She opened the stall door. "Hi, Radish! You ready to play?"

Radish whirled away and ducked his head into the corner of the stall. Rae went toward him with the halter, but he turned again, blocking her with his butt.

In stories, Rae loved bratty ponies. In real life, this was embarrassing and a little hurtful. She knew better than to keep chasing him. She looked over the half door, hoping to catch Tish's eye.

But Tish was helping Steve, and Judy was talking seriously with Amber as they led Princess out of her stall. What a beautiful pony! She was like Guillaume, though, polite and distant. Maybe all perfect ponies were like that—

Something poked her back. Rae jumped and turned. Radish stood gazing at her with soft, bright eyes.

"Gotcha!" She wrapped the lead rope around his neck so he couldn't get away, and put on the halter. She'd read that you could catch ponies by ignoring them. Eventually they got curious and came close. She hadn't done it on purpose, but it had worked.

So good, she'd overcome a challenge already, and Radish's

sparkling eyes were making her laugh. "I like naughty ponies," she told Radish. "We're going to have fun!"

She saddled him and led him out to the ring with everyone else.

"Intermediates, mount up and ride to the far end of the ring," Tish said. "Use the mounting block to get on. It's better for the ponies' backs."

When it was her turn, Rae lined Radish up beside the mounting block. She wasn't sure he would cooperate. His small muzzle twitched with mischief. But he stood still, letting Rae slip into the saddle.

She was *on*! On *Radish*, and riding him toward the intermediate end of the ring.

do i know you?

PRINCESS'S legs felt zingier with every passing minute—the kids, the noise, the unpredictability. Now Amber was on her back, scared, and pretending not to be. She twitched and gasped every time Princess turned her head.

Tish had them circle their half of the ring. That was like a show, at least, and Amber did know how to ride. But she felt terrible up there, like she was made of wood. Princess did exactly as she was asked, and Amber didn't seem to hear her grinding her teeth.

~

"RAE, that's looking good!" Tish said.

It *felt* good. Rae sat just the way she did on Rusty, straight and centered. *Thank you, Dad!* All that practicing had paid off. The only differences were Radish's jouncy step and his tiny sharp ears pricking this way and that, following his busy thoughts.

Something felt unconnected, though, like a car without a steering wheel. Were her reins too long? She peeked at the other kids. Their reins seemed shorter than hers, but when she tried to make an adjustment, Radish pulled them through her hands and unadjusted them. He wanted them long. So that had to be right, right? She shouldn't make him uncomfortable—

Tish said, "In a minute I'm going to have you trot. Shorten—"

Too late. Radish knew that word. He took off trotting faster than Rae had ever ridden before, blasting past all the other ponies. Rae bobbed up and down, loosening in the saddle. Her teeth rattled and her eyes blurred.

"Rae, shorten your reins!" Tish called. Rae barely heard. They flashed past Princess, who whipped her head around, making a vicious face. The image burned into Rae's brain— silver ears buried in a gray foam of mane, jaws wide, teeth bared—*afraid*. Princess was afraid . . .

"Radish, *WHOA!*"

Tish's voice was like a thunderclap. Radish didn't exactly whoa, but he did slow down.

Shorten your reins! The command caught up to Rae's brain. She hauled them in till she had contact with the bit, and Radish stopped.

"Well ridden!" Tish said. "You didn't even lose a stirrup, Rae!"

The ring seemed to be spinning slightly. Rae checked on herself. She was still on. She did have both feet in the stirrups. So that was all right—

"You okay, Amber?" Tish asked. Amber nodded, barely. She

158

had pulled Princess to a halt. Princess's neck was high and tight, and they both looked upset.

Tish walked over to Rae and Radish. In a more private voice she said, "I noticed that you didn't try to stop him, Rae. Exactly how much riding experience have you had?"

"I've had . . . three lessons. And I've watched a lot."

"The three lessons were ones you had with me?" Tish's eyebrows rose. "You looked so great in the saddle, I assumed you'd ridden quite a bit. You don't have a pony at home?"

Rae was *not* going to mention Rusty. She was just not. "No. I've read books."

"Well you've learned more from them than most people!" Tish said. "But no rider with only three lessons under her belt can manage Radish in a setting like this. Time for a swap."

Rae's heart sank. "No—" she started to say, but Tish was looking around at the group.

"Amber, bring Princess over here. She needs to go to the quiet end of the ring, and Radish needs to be reminded that people are in charge. You rode him last year. Were you in control?"

"By the end," Amber said, brightening.

"Let's see if you can manage that two years in a row. It's been the making of many a rider! Rae, take Princess over to work with Judy."

Rae got off Radish. Her face felt hot. Tish was making it seem like this was all about what the ponies needed. But really it was about her not knowing enough and saying she was intermediate when really she was a beginner. Now she was losing Radish. Already. She wanted to ask, *Please can I keep him?* But she'd spent a long time learning not to ask, when she knew the answer would be no.

Her face may have asked, though. Tish paused. "This feels like a demotion, doesn't it? I'm sorry. That's my fault. I should have asked more questions. But I need your help, Rae. Princess is fragile, more fragile than I realized when I put her in my program. Look at her muzzle—see how pinched it is? Her nostrils aren't even flaring. It's like she's holding her breath, trying not to be here."

Rae understood. Right now she would rather not be here either.

"Being a lesson pony has turned out to be stressful for her," Tish said. "Things will be calmer at the other end of the ring. That will be good for Princess—and good for you too, Rae. You're a new rider, in spite of how well you sit. You need to start where you are, not where you'd like to be."

That was what Eden's instructor had said, but Tish said it kindly, and that helped Rae understand. It was just something that was true, not something to feel bad about.

But she wasn't quite there yet. "I love Radish," she found herself saying.

Tish smiled. "How could you not? Come on, I'll give you a leg up."

In a moment Rae was in the saddle. Princess was taller than Radish. Rae could easily see over the top rail of the fence.

"Go ahead, ride over there," Tish said. "You don't need me to escort you. Take care of each other, you two!"

Rae turned her head toward the beginners' group. Princess

turned with her and started walking. This would be the longest ride Rae had ever taken without being supervised, she realized. Right after being run away with, too. She must not be completely hopeless, if Tish had turned her loose like that.

But Radish! She had loved his lively, prancing walk. Princess had a completely different gait, long and strong and purposeful, a smooth glide that ate up the distance—

—and okay, that was wonderful. Rae had had dreams that felt like this . . .

~

PRINCESS had rarely felt this jangled. Her legs wanted to prance—no, *gallop*, all the way back to the quiet of her stall.

But that wasn't possible. People were in charge, even people like this Rae-girl. At least she wasn't as wooden as the last girl. She wasn't afraid, and she held the reins lightly. Princess was able to stretch her neck long, open up her stride. They threaded between the jumps dividing the ring and headed toward where the other group of ponies were all standing in a half circle.

~

"RAE, welcome!" Judy said. "Another Radish survivor. You get a T-shirt! Seriously, we had some printed up!"

Rae looked down, embarrassed. It was strange to be welcomed like a hero after what just happened.

"We're starting with some exercises," Judy said. "I call it Pony Yoga. The first one is the most important—Child Pose.

"Let your reins lie loosely on your pony's neck, everybody. Now, lean forward, all the way. Pretend you're giving that pony a big hug. Reach your arms as far down his shoulders as you can.

161

"Now relax. Let your arms drape over your pony and just lie there. Feel the sun on your back. Feel your pony's mane on your cheek and his shoulders holding you up. Yes, Steve, that big bump on the front of the saddle does get in the way. See if you can soften your body over the top of it.

"Excellent. Can you feel your pony take a breath in? He lifts your arms and drops your arms, but always he holds you up. You're melting into him . . ."

Princess's breath wasn't easy to feel. Rae remembered her pinched nostrils. Poor Princess! It didn't seem right to even ride her if it was going to make her this tense.

But could Rae ever have relaxed like this on Radish?

Without meaning to, she let out a sigh.

⁓

PRINCESS stopped breathing completely for a few seconds. What did the girl mean by that sound? Had something startled her?

But out of Princess's belly came an answering sigh. Her breath understood. It came deeper, larger. A new feeling began to flow into her, warmth and comfort, like the feeling of that dog-smelling blanket on her first day here. Like the feeling of the old man's hands and her mother's breath.

Did it come from this girl? Nothing else had changed, so feeling better must have something to do with Rae.

"Feel your heart beating," Judy said. "Feel the warmth of your pony's body. Feel the two of you becoming one."

⁓

RAE did feel it. Her heart was pressed against Princess, and a long ache, the longest of her life, was eased.

Judy said, "Your pony's got your back, and you've got his. You want the best for each other. Knowing that, sit up slowly and open your eyes."

Rae did. There was a momentary dizzy feeling, like when Radish had stopped trotting. She took hold of the front of the saddle, and Princess turned her head. Suddenly Rae was looking into Princess's large, dark eye.

Everything stopped inside her. She stared, caught out of time . . .

I *know* you.

Do I know you?

chapter 32

the
rae-girl

RAE had no time to think about that strange moment of recognition. Judy led them in more exercises. Standing in the stirrups. Holding both hands out to the sides. Touching the ponies' ears and tails. Reaching down to touch their own toes.

Through it all Princess stood still, struggling to understand. All this wiggling! What was it for? Couldn't they go back to the part where Rae lay still and the two of them breathed? Princess could keep that up for a long time. She could do this too, but it wasn't as nice, with Rae all anxious and elbowy.

The last exercise was Around the World. Judy had the kids turn around so they were sitting backward in their saddles, then to keep on going till they faced front again. Then back the other way, over and over. "This is to loosen you up and give you confidence," she said.

It was jiggly and annoying, but when Princess couldn't

help taking a step, Judy came to stand at her head and Rae kept going, around and around. She got smoother at it. Her hands found chances to give Princess a warm pat, and Princess's legs found the way to stand still again. Judy stepped away.

"Now let's make it a race," she said. "Everyone face front, with your feet in your stirrups. When I say *go*, head off around the world. First one with their feet back in the stirrups wins. Ready, set, go!"

Rae slipped her feet out of the stirrups and whirled herself around. In seconds she was facing front again, feeling for the stirrups. For some people that was the hard part, but Rae had had plenty of practice finding her stirrups on Rusty. "Done!" she said.

The others were still finishing. She looked toward the intermediate half of the ring. She saw Radish, trotting so fast that Amber's blond hair stood straight out behind her. He blasted past Banner and Asterix, and then Amber turned him in a tight circle, bringing him under control.

So that was what Rae should have done. To her surprise, she didn't want to be over there doing it. She rested one hand on Princess's withers, just in front of the saddle. A silver ear tipped back at her.

Yes. This was fine.

The next lesson was on dismounting. Judy got on Princess to demonstrate. "Feet, out of stirrups. Reins, dropped on your pony's neck. Hands, on his withers. Lean forward, swing your legs up, and vault off—bending your knees as you land. And lift your reins over his head, ready to lead him away."

Everyone practiced. "Feet!" "Reins!" "Hands!" "Vault!"

Princess wasn't liking this much. Rae could read that in the crinkles near her eyes, the tense set of her ears. "Sorry," she said, every time her feet slapped the ground.

"We'll end the lesson with a race," Judy said. "When I say go, everyone do a proper dismount. Ready, set . . ."

Rae heard something odd—a gritty, rasping sound. She leaned forward. What was that? ". . . go!" she heard, just as she realized Princess was grinding her teeth.

"I win!" Steve crowed.

Rae just sat there, gently stroking Princess's short mane so it lay flat on one side of her neck. "It's all right," she murmured. "It's all right. You're a good, good girl."

"Everything okay, Rae?" Judy asked.

"Princess hates this," Rae explained. "She's grinding her teeth."

"Good job noticing that!" Judy said. "Sometimes this pony is too well-behaved for her own good. I'll stand at her head while you get off."

Rae slid out of the saddle, slowly and softly.

"You can head to the barn," Judy said.

Rae walked beside Princess. Amber was ahead of her leading Radish, who was all sweated up and pleased with himself. Rae glanced sidelong at Princess. Her eyes were wide and strained.

"Hey," Rae said, putting the flat of her hand on Princess's neck as they walked. "Don't stress."

Princess heaved a sigh and lowered her head as that sense of comfort began to flow again. There was something different about this Rae-girl. Good different, like spring coming, or a pasture gate opening.

Tish and Judy supervised untacking and handed out carrots from a big plastic bag for the riders to give as treats. Sweaty intermediate ponies were walked cool. Beginner ponies, who'd been standing around all afternoon, were put into their stalls, and Judy showed everyone how to read the charts that told what to feed them.

Rae double-checked and triple-checked Princess's directions, and then asked Judy. It didn't seem right that Princess should get such a tiny amount of grain after all she'd been through.

"We have to watch her weight," Judy said. "Her body adapted to being starved, so she gets fat very easily. Ponies do that anyway. So yes, that's the right amount."

Rae dumped the grain in Princess's bucket and watched her eat it fiercely, biting so hard her teeth scraped the bottom of the bucket. Was she afraid there might not be more grain, ever? Rae rushed upstairs to fill the hay net. There shouldn't be even a second when Princess didn't have something to eat.

She hung the net and turned to find Princess watching her with wide, dark eyes. Rae said, "I'm your person for the next three weeks. Is that okay? You still have Tish, but I'll feed you supper and ride you and . . . I hope I do a good job."

Princess listened to the rise and fall of the soft voice. The Rae-girl was not as self-confident as her other girls. Still, there was that peace around her, and a sweetness.

Did it matter? Girls were a one- or two-day experience. Princess reached past Rae to snatch a bite from the hay net.

Rae walked out of the barn and found Gammer waiting in her truck. "How was your first day?" Gammer asked, when

Rae was seat-belted in and they were heading up the driveway.

"Yes," Rae said, staring straight ahead.

"Was it good?" Gammer asked.

"Oh. I think . . ."

Was it good? Rae closed her eyes. Radish . . . and the runaway, or trot-away . . . and Princess . . . What did it mean, that look of recognition? Her heart still felt bruised about Radish. But behind her eyelids what she saw was Princess.

here
we go!

RAE slept all the way home and went to bed right after supper. By morning she was able to talk, and things became clearer as everyone asked questions.

"So you ride well, actually?"

"No, Dad, I *sit* well. Thanks to Rusty."

"She likes Rusty?"

"Well—I'm sure she would. If I told her about him."

"And things didn't go as you expected." That was Gammer, as they drove along the winding road to Tish's stable. "Good! If you knew what to expect, you wouldn't be learning. Do you like Princess?"

Rae hesitated. That moment of recognition still puzzled her. Princess had been so quiet, not nudgy and nippy like Radish. She hid her feelings.

"So not love at first sight, then," Gammer said. "Good. I've been afraid that you'd get too attached."

"Mmm," Rae said. *Did* she like Princess? *Of course!* was one answer. Princess was a pony. And *maybe not* was another, because in a way, Princess was more like a picture of a pony, an extremely beautiful one that Rae would have loved to have on her wall—but flat, not letting her feelings show . . .

Except they did show. Rae had felt Princess's fear, her jangled nerves, her fierce hunger, and something else, in that quiet moment during Pony Yoga. "I don't know," she said.

Gammer looked over at her with a smile. "That question was five miles ago, my dear!"

~

Today when the campers arrived the ponies were all in their stalls, finishing their hay. Princess turned from her net and gave Rae a long, penetrating look.

Okay, what did *that* mean? *You came back*, was what popped into Rae's mind. She thought Princess looked surprised. "Hi," Rae said. "Yes, it's me."

Princess breathed a light, purring snort and reached for the last wisp of hay. Pleased? Rae thought she might be.

But it was a difficult day. Judy got the beginners actually riding—making the ponies move by squeezing with their legs, making them stop by tightening the reins, making them turn by tightening just one rein.

Rae listened hard and tried to do exactly what she was told. It was challenging, though. Every time she tightened a rein, one of Princess's ears would tip back. It was a

170

comment. Not snarky. Princess was never snarky. But she seemed slightly pained. By the end of the morning lesson Rae felt clumsy and incompetent, like a little kid trying to cut paper with kindergarten scissors.

At lunch, Judy took Rae aside. "You're overcueing her," she said.

Rae just stared. What did that even mean?

"She doesn't need you to shout at her with the reins," Judy said. "She can hear you whisper. Look, everybody else is on a school pony. Those guys are not going to take a single step unless somebody makes them. But with Princess you can use your reins lightly. She'll understand. So try this. When I tell the others to turn right, you *look* right. See if that's enough."

At first it wasn't. During the afternoon lesson when Judy asked them to turn, Rae glanced to her right. Princess kept going straight.

"Not just your eyes, Rae," Judy called. "Turn your head."

Turn your *head* . . . Rae did, and Princess turned right. The tipped-back ear seemed approving, not critical. Oh! Rae turned her head, and turned, and turned—

"Now the other way," Judy suggested, and they spiraled off to the left. This was amazing! It must be what writers meant when they talked about being at one with your horse. Princess was coming to life beneath her, softening and smoothing out after a day that had seemed all corners and elbows . . .

Princess felt the tension release from her neck. Lovely! Rae did know something about riding after all. She was waking up and starting to speak with her body, starting to understand what she was doing. A feeling of joy came from her, the kind of joy Princess expected from a girl.

~

After supper Rae went out into the yard and climbed onto Rusty.

"Ow." She had some sore muscles. She positioned herself in the saddle and looked out between Rusty's wild garden-trowel ears. She'd taken some fine imaginary rides on him. Now when she patted his bristly neck, she could feel that he was just a thing—a wonderful, helpful, funny thing, but all Rae could think about was Princess.

~

Princess wanted every single oat of her breakfast, every single grain pellet. She chased the last ones around the bottom of her bucket. But her ears kept pricking toward the door. Tish and Judy had fed the ponies early again. That must mean the children were coming for the third day in a row. Would Rae?

At last she heard an engine sound. A truck door slammed. "You're early!" Tish said.

"Is that okay? Gammer has pies to deliver—"

Rae! Princess thrust her head over the stall door. "Is she the one who makes those pies?" Judy was asking. "I *love* those pies!"

Rae appeared in the big doorway. A nicker burst from Princess's throat. *You're here!* It was nothing she meant to say. It said itself.

"*Princess!*" Rae said, coming closer. Princess pushed her muzzle up to Rae's cheek, drawing in a scent of sugar and strawberries and Rae-ness.

Rae stood very still. "What is she doing?"

"She's greeting you," Tish said quietly. "I've only seen her do that with one other person—my nephew Bill, who rescued her."

Rae's hands crept up to the sides of Princess's neck. "Hello, Princess," she whispered. "Hello."

"Oh boy," Tish murmured, somewhere behind her. "Here we go!"

chapter 34

pining

That moment changed everything. Even time changed. For Rae, each ride on Princess seemed to last hours, yet the first week of camp sped by in ten minutes.

By then Rae and Princess had already passed many milestones. Because Rae sat so beautifully, thanks to the hours on Rusty, balanced above the balls of her feet in perfect alignment, she was able to pick up posting—rising in her stirrups at every other trot stride—in one lesson. When the beginners played Follow the Leader, Rae and Princess were the leaders.

There were other games. Egg and Spoon, where Rae had to carry a hard-boiled egg on a spoon while riding. (The old dog obligingly cleaned up after that one.) Ribbon Race, where two riders went side by side, holding a length of ribbon between them. Simon Says. Musical Grain Bags.

The other ponies had experienced these games many

times. Not Princess. Rings were for going around and around, sweetly and sedately, and afterward collecting a blue ribbon. In this ring eggs fell off spoons, paper ribbons ripped, music played, and when it stopped, Rae would aim her at a grain bag on the ground, trying to get there before another pony could. It made no sense—but since Rae wanted to, Princess did it. Rae wanted to ride side by side with another pony; that was harder, and Princess's dragon faces were not an asset, but they tried and didn't always fail.

Friday afternoon Tish took Rae aside. "I want you back in intermediates. Princess is very experienced, and you're getting there. You've missed the cantering lessons, but Princess knows the verbal cue, and she won't use it against you like Radish would! When I give the cue to get ready, sit deep and let your outside leg slide back. I'll say 'canter,' and she'll canter. You just go with her."

It happened as Tish said it would. At the word *canter* Princess lifted like a merry-go-round horse, smooth and rhythmic. But unlike on a merry-go-round, Rae felt the powerful potential to go forward at speed. It was like a dream, riding a long rippling rhythm that Rae knew already, deep in her bones. It was the best part of the week, for Princess as well as Rae.

But on the next two days, Rae didn't come.

Princess felt the jangles in her legs again. She roamed her stall and paddock, always looking toward the driveway, always listening. No Rae. Was she like all the other girls, like the old man?

"You're pining, Princess," Tish said. "Don't worry. She'll be back Monday."

Those were sounds Princess didn't understand. But the third day Judy and Tish fed everyone early again. Princess ignored the grain in her pail. This was the pattern. Did it mean . . . She heard an engine sound she knew, a familiar door slam, and then a figure appeared in the barn doorway. Princess let out a loud whinny.

Tish turned and stared. "Princess! You've hardly made a peep since you got here!"

Rae was at the stall already. "She's not eating her grain, Tish. Is she sick—no, wait, now she's eating."

"She was waiting for you," Tish said.

The second week was even better than the first. Lots of cantering. Trail rides through the woods around Tish's stable. Faster afternoon games, including Sit-a-Buck (holding a dollar bill under your leg while riding), Flag Race, and No Hands (riding a simple pattern with the reins lying on the pony's neck). For Rae and Princess, No Hands was especially easy.

"Now you can see why we work on sitting in alignment," Tish said. "Rae's legs and weight can speak to Princess because she's always in the right place. We ride this way because it's effective, not because it's pretty. Amber, you're up next."

"I wonder where I'll *end* up," Amber said. But with reminders to focus on her balance and to steer with her thighs and seat, she guided Radish through almost as good a test as Princess's. "After this I'll always ride him without reins!" she said proudly.

"And *that's* why we play games!" Tish said.

The wildest game was Broom Polo—like soccer, only the players rode ponies, and instead of kicking the ball, they hit it with brooms. Getting that close to so many running ponies seemed like a terrible idea to Princess, but Rae seemed to want that ball, so she went after it, flattening her ears when other ponies got in the way. They pretty much ignored her, and that was good. Gradually, she was learning to ignore them too.

By the end of the week, the intermediates started learning to jump. Princess had only ever jumped the field brook and the fallen log and that one little fence with Tish. Rae had never ridden a pony over a jump even once, though she'd watched Eden do it countless times. But they were both fearless, and they learned quickly. Each jump felt better than the last, better than almost anything else. For both of them.

And then it was Friday again. How did that happen? At home, Rae looked at her calendar. One week left. One week.

She turned the calendar to the wall.

~

In a nursing home miles away, a thin, tremulous old man had recovered enough that his niece felt bound to tell him what she'd concealed all these months. She prepared the nursing staff to be ready to help. What she had to say would be a shock.

"Uncle, a bad thing happened after you got sick. Darlene called me every week or so for months, telling me everything was fine at Highover, and I—I believed her."

His eyes went wide, fixed on her face.

"Now it seems foolish, but I knew you trusted her and Charlie . . . and they . . . they left the ponies to starve. Two boys found them, just in time."

His eyes were almost popping out of his head. "Pnccss?" he hissed.

"They all lived," Ms. Calloway said quickly. "They're all

quite healthy now. In fact, the one that was sickest is being used at a riding school."

"Psssss!"

"I'm so sorry, I don't understand. I've asked the nurse to prepare a sedative for you. I knew this would be a shock. But the important thing to remember is that they are all fine—"

"*PCCSSSS?*"

~

"You've hardly said two words all day," Gammer said on Saturday evening. "Are you pining?"

Rae couldn't answer. That cherry-pit lump was back in her throat, and this time it was stuck. Monday seemed forever away.

"Tell you what," Gammer said. "I have pies to deliver over that way tomorrow morning. Why don't you ride along with me, and we'll stop and visit Princess."

Rae couldn't answer that either, except with a hug.

The next morning, they pulled into Tish's place. Princess, out for her short grazing session, lifted her head from the grass. "Is that her?" Gammer asked.

But she was talking to Rae's back. Two seconds later Rae had ducked under the fence. Princess came to meet her, and they sniffed noses, catching the scent of each other's breakfasts— grass for Princess, pancakes with butter and maple syrup for Rae.

Tish pushed a wheelbarrow around the corner and paused, wiping sweat off her forehead. "Oh, hi, Rae. Are you here to visit? Judy has weekends off, and I'm cleaning stalls."

"I'll clean Princess's stall," Rae said. "Please?"

Tish laughed. "Be my guest!"

"How long will it take?" Gammer asked. "I can stay for a few minutes, but I have a lot of baking to do this afternoon."

"If Rae wants to stay and help with stalls, I'll happily bring her home afterward," Tish said.

Rae cleaned Princess's stall, and three others too. Then, while Tish did some organizing in the grain room, she groomed Princess. When she was done, she just sat in the corner of the fresh, pine-scented stall and watched Princess eat hay. Tish found her there half an hour later.

"You'd move in if you could, wouldn't you? But right now, I'd better get you home."

On the drive, Rae found herself telling Tish the story of her life: Mom's accident, Gammer's apartment, Dad's garbage truck and sculptures, and Rusty.

"Oh, *that's* why you sit so well! I need a Rusty. Will you show him to me?" So at home Rae introduced her to Dad, who led her around the back side of the house. Tish burst out laughing.

"You didn't tell me he was a work of art! I have some old machinery at the stable. Would you like to come see if there's a Rusty in there? And how much would you charge?"

Rae's father looked as bug-eyed as Rusty for a moment. "I'll—I don't—"

"He'll work up a quote," Rae said.

"Excellent!" Tish said. She stood looking at the weary old barn, the small grassy area, the berry bushes and apple trees. "What a super place!" she said. "Thank you for your help, Rae. I'll see you tomorrow morning."

chapter 35

distractions

The last week of camp was the longest, six days instead of five. It would end on Saturday, after the show.

All the campers would ride in it, but few would win ribbons, Tish warned. Good riders and fine horses from miles around competed at this show. The school ponies excelled at teaching, not showing. Still, each year one or two campers did get ribbons.

But ribbons weren't the point, said Tish. The point was learning. Getting ready to compete, they would develop new skills and perfect the ones they already had. They would sit better, post better, stop better, jump better. That was the real prize, not a little piece of silk ribbon.

They all agreed. Of course, it was all about learning. But the word *ribbon* was on everyone's lips, and it made things happen. Steve actually got Nubbin to canter. Lori learned to get on Banner by herself. Then she learned to do it gracefully. Amber was able to slow Radish down sometimes. When she couldn't, she was able to keep a serene, I'm-doing-this-on-purpose expression on her face as he trotted pell-mell around the ring.

Rae worked hardest of all. She and Princess practiced jumping. They practiced show-ring maneuvers—the correct way to reverse directions, the proper way to stand in a lineup. Princess knew them all by heart, but they were new to Rae.

Most of all they practiced being passed by other ponies. "The judge will really take off points for those faces she makes," Tish said. "We should be able to train her out of it. It seems like a habit more than anything else at this point."

She had Amber ride Radish past Rae and Princess again and again. As Princess turned her head, Rae was supposed to hold the reins firmly, so Princess would bump against the bit. "You aren't pulling her mouth," Tish said. "*She's* pulling. She's smart enough to figure it out."

Rae was rather wimpy about holding the reins firm. Nonetheless, Princess did figure it out. Fine. She didn't need to whip her whole head around to make a dragon face. She could flatten her ears, roll her eyes, and show her teeth, while keeping her neck in a straight line.

"It's . . . somewhat better," Tish said. "Keep her going at a good brisk clip. Maybe nobody will pass you. Hope is everything when it comes to shows. And a sense of humor."

The other campers were dreaming up what they'd do for costume class. Steve wanted to turn Nubbin into a couch. Amber brought in large, leafy radish tops made out of green paper to turn Radish into his namesake vegetable. Other kids had other ideas, some that would even work.

This was one of those times when Rae felt like an outsider. She was too serious. She'd focused completely on Princess, not at all on the other kids, and now she couldn't think of a single thing she would want to turn Princess into. Just leading her into the ring, her unadorned self, with a sign that said *Most Beautiful Pony*—that wasn't a costume.

"Not everybody goes in costume," Tish reassured her. "Just like not everybody goes in the jumping class—though Steve is determined to try! But I want you to enter that if you feel like it, Rae. You have everything to learn about making it look pretty, but for a jumping class, all you need is a fast, clean round. Are you up for that?"

For jumping on Princess? Rae didn't have the words for how up for it she was. She could only nod.

⁓

At home Rae didn't talk much. She thought about Princess, and the end of camp, and . . . then what? Back to normal? That was impossible. She was a different person now, somebody whose days had been filled, for almost three weeks, with ponies. A pony. *The* pony. How could she go back to the same life after that?

And how could Princess? She had been a lesson pony, but that hadn't suited her. So what next? Back to Highover? Tish had said the ponies still lived there, now managed by someone the owner's relative had hired. Princess could be returned to the farm, perhaps to a tiny grassy paddock like she had at Tish's.

And if that was all the future held for her, why couldn't she come here, to the tiny grassy area in Rae's own backyard?

She tried not to ask herself that. There had always been a reason before, every time she'd thought that now, or soon, they would be able to manage a pony. The truck broke. The roof needed repairs. But she did have a bank account these days, and a business. She should ask . . .

She couldn't make herself. The answer would probably be no, and she would still have the last few days of camp to get through, and the show. Better to wait, keep the hope tiny and hidden, and when camp was over bring it out and see if it survived.

But since she was determined not to say what was on her mind, she hardly said anything. Dad and Gammer kept looking at her with worried expressions, and going off to discuss something privately. "Not *if*," she heard Gammer say once. "*How?*"

Good question. How would Rae make herself ask? How would she be able to endure the answer? How could she ever love any pony as much as she loved Princess? She lay awake for hours every night, trying not to wonder.

The long week, the last week, came to an end with one final jumping lesson Friday morning. Tish focused on controlling the approach. That wasn't easy. "Clearly, jumping is one thing Princess *wasn't* trained to do," Tish said. "She's working on raw talent and enthusiasm. Do you love it as much as she does?"

Rae nodded. "It's scary, but—" But there came a moment when they were flying, just the two of them, when Princess's hoofbeats went silent and Rae folded down over her neck, stretching her hands forward. They were one, with no choices to make. Then Princess's hooves touched down, and Rae had to guide her again, to the next jump. Yes, she loved that as much as Princess did, and the lesson seemed far too short.

Friday afternoon the campers washed their ponies, cleaned tack, and chose riding coats from Tish's secondhand collection. Then Tish handed around entry forms and explained what classes they could go in: for Rae and Princess there were five—halter, equitation, pleasure, trail, and jumping.

"Are we good enough for jumping?" Rae asked.

"For this class you are," Tish said. "All you have to do is get over the fences without any refusals or knocked-down rails. Everybody who has a clear round goes in the jump-off, and that's judged on speed."

"We made the jump-off last year," Amber said. "It was a blast!"

"It's a very popular class," Tish said. "There's always a big crowd for jumping. Any questions on your forms?" She leaned over Rae's shoulder. "I'm not Princess's owner, Rae. Cross my name out and put *Roland McDermott*."

Roland McDermott. That was the old man who owned Highover, the one who got sick. "Is he—" *Still alive*, Rae wanted to ask.

"He's getting better, from what I hear. He's well enough that his niece finally told him what happened to the ponies. She'd kept that from him until now."

He must feel terrible, Rae thought, as she printed his name on her entry form. It hadn't been his fault, except that he trusted the wrong people. He would blame himself for that. She knew she would. It was good that he was getting better, though.

Better enough to want his pony back?

Now it was time to feed; the last feeding. This was the last day she would carry the tiny amount of grain into Princess's stall, the last day she would fill the hay net—unless she dared to ask. Even thinking of it made her heart pound. The thing about asking was, you got an answer. Rae leaned against Princess's side, breathing in her clean scent, listening to her munch hay. She never wanted to move again.

But Tish wanted them all to gather. When everyone was at the picnic tables, she made a little speech. Visualize success, she suggested. Not ribbons—those were up to someone else's judgment. *Success* was up to each of them. Staying calm, paying attention to details, being safe—those were all things they could control, and if they managed all or most of them, they would have something to be proud of tomorrow.

"So get a good night's sleep," Tish finished. "Don't let distractions in—most of them will keep. You've all worked hard and so have the ponies. Tomorrow is your chance to use what you've learned. Not for a ribbon. For these animals. Most of them come from humble origins. They won't be the most beautiful ponies at the show. But do them proud, and they'll do the same for you."

Princess didn't come from humble origins, Rae thought, and she *would* be the most beautiful pony—though her mane still stuck straight up in places, and she'd have to wear a red ribbon in her tail, and there was the scar . . . no, Tish was right. This was no time for distractions—so don't think about camp ending. Don't think about Sunday, and next week, and asking Dad, and his answer. *Focus.*

185

Rae hardly said a word on the way home. She ate supper—without tasting it—and went upstairs to get her clothes ready. She borrowed a raggy old shirt of Dad's to keep her good things clean, laid out the jacket from Tish's collection, and brought out the one pair of Mom's riding pants that finally, nearly, fit. They were a dark brick-orange, not a fashionable color. Mom must have bought them on closeout and she'd worn them a lot, but they were neatly mended. The belt held them in place even though they were a tiny bit too big.

Rae put everything in a pile near the door, beside her riding boots and helmet. She took a shower, got into pajamas, and headed for bed. *Get a good night's sleep.* Ha! Passing the window, she decided not to look out. This was no time to try to see Princess out there. *Don't let distractions—*

But who was that, moving around in the moonlight? Dad. He stood staring at the grassy area, the paddock place, scratching his chin. Now he started pacing it off, walking in short steps and counting to himself. But why was he measuring it? He would never build anything there, not even a garden bed. He had promised. It was the pony paddock—

It was the pony paddock.

Like fireworks, the tingling birthday feeling exploded inside Rae. Not the realistic feeling of recent birthdays; this was the feeling from long-ago birthdays when she'd believed, truly believed, that this could be the year. She remembered Gammer's long talk with Tish last weekend, how Tish had nodded so approvingly when she saw the barn and backyard. Gammer saying, "Not *if. How.*"

Rae felt her heart start to gallop. It all added up. The best thing for Princess, the best thing for her—

She turned in a circle, almost dizzy, and saw the pile of riding clothes. *Don't let distraction in.*

This was the biggest distraction of all. She owed it to Princess to go to bed, and go to sleep.

ribbons

PRINCESS was finishing the hay Rae had given her when she noticed unusual activity in the barn. Tish and Judy were packing up tack and grooming kits, piling hay bales near the door, checking lists. Why would they be doing that? This was like the days after the ambulance came and woke the gnawing feeling in Princess's belly.

On Saturday morning breakfast came early, before the sun was up. Soon several horse trailers and a big truck pulled into the yard, and everything staged near the door was loaded into them. Ignoring the hay in her net, Princess watched over her stall door as the other ponies were led out. She heard them thud up trailer ramps.

Then it was her turn; down the aisle of the empty barn, into a trailer next to Nubbin. The truck started, and with a gentle *whoosh* the trailer began to roll. Old memories stirred. Girls, blue ribbons, the trainer's false voice, and the old man's gentle hands. Brown sugar. Was that where she was going? She snatched a mouthful of hay from the net and munched it, remembering.

She'd finished about a third of the hay when the trailer slowed and made a careful turn. The way the floor dipped under Princess's hooves, the angle of the trailer, felt familiar. She had been here before. She turned her head, trying to see out the slanted windows.

The trailer parked. The doors opened. Tish untied her and backed her down the ramp.

Princess turned and stood, head high, staring. That barn, that row of stalls, the ring with the white gazebo beside it— she'd seen them before, hadn't she? But everything looked different from up here at the edge of the big field. Tish tied her to the trailer next to Nubbin. Princess turned as far as the rope would let her, to gaze, to sniff the air.

This *was* the right place.

He should be here.

And Tish, Judy, and all Tish's horses were here, so *Rae* should be here—

And there she was hurrying across the grass in a baggy shirt and riding pants, followed by that old woman who smelled like ripe fruit and an unfamiliar man. Princess whinnied. Rae rushed to her, and Princess lifted her muzzle to Rae's cheek.

"I see what you mean!" Dad said to Gammer.

"Oh good, you're here, Rae," Tish said. "You don't look as if you slept much, in spite of my wise advice! Let's take Princess on a tour before the others get here. For all we know this is her first show ever." She untied the rope. "I'll handle her till we see how she is."

Princess walked with a high head, her eyes wide and bright. "She seems bigger," Rae said.

"They do, at shows," Tish said. "It's the excitement. She's behaving like royalty, though." She handed the rope to Rae, but stayed close, watching, until the other campers started to arrive. "I'd say we have an experienced pony here. Bring her back— whoops! Steve, wait!" She rushed off to the trailers.

Rae followed. Everything looked grainy and out of focus this morning, like an old movie. She'd hardly slept at all last night. She tied Princess to the trailer again and brushed her dappled sides till they shone like pewter candlesticks, combed out every tangle from her tail, smoothed the short, bouncy mane over to one side with a damp brush. It would not lie flat, no matter what she did, and neither would the hairs on Princess's chest. She would always be marked by that long, slashing scar.

Giving up, Rae braided a bright red ribbon into Princess's tail. Princess wouldn't kick, but this would help other riders avoid the dragon faces. As she worked, Rae was aware of Dad and Gammer watching her, speaking to each other. She couldn't hear what they were saying.

"Campers! Ten minutes till showtime," Tish called. "Stop grooming ponies and start grooming yourselves!"

Rae pulled off Dad's big shirt, tucked her good shirt in, and tightened the belt with the hoof-pick buckle. "Do I look okay, Gammer?"

"Just like your mama!" Gammer helped Rae into the borrowed riding coat and pinned on her number. Near them a black box hissed and crackled to life.

"*Good morning, everyone. This is Abby Portchester welcoming*

you to the Sixteenth Annual Pleasant Valley Shelter Benefit Horse
Show. Visit the shelter booth sometime during the day to see what
good work they've been up to lately and, of course, donate."

Rae smoothed her hand protectively along Princess's neck.

"This will be the first call for halter class. Contestants, please
make your way to the ring."

They were all in halter class, and they walked down together,
Radish tugging Amber and Steve tugging Nubbin, Banner
prancing around high-headed as if he'd never been to a show
before. Rae, behind them, felt a sudden clutch in her throat. It
wasn't just Princess she'd be missing—might be missing—next
week.

As they got nearer to the ring, Princess seemed to grow even
taller. She gazed at the spectators along the rail, hardly seeming
to notice that Rae was there. Rae gazed at them too. So many
people. She'd known there would be. It was a show, after all. But
she hadn't thought about what it would be like to be in the ring
in front of all those eyes.

The announcer was saying something. Rae knew all the
words. What did they mean, though? Her mind had suddenly
gone all scrambly.

Princess understood exactly what they meant. This was a
show, a simple place where only certain things happened. She
knew them all. Halter classes always came early, while the mists
were still rising off the showground, and were always the same.
Circle the ring in both directions at a flat-footed walk. Line up
facing the ringmaster, feet squared up tidily. Stand perfectly still,
gazing regally off over the crowd. Rae was the only difference,
not in exactly the right place. The old man had always stood

slightly farther away, the lead looping long between them. He hadn't stared at the crowd the way Rae was doing. Instead he'd gazed proudly at Princess.

The judge made her slow way down the line, looking sharply at horses and ponies, checking the undersides of halter straps for dirt, making marks on her clipboard. When she reached Princess, she jotted something down, then looked up abruptly, frowning. "I could swear I know this pony. Beautiful animal! Too bad about the scar. Trot her out for me, please."

Rae stood rooted to the spot. Her eyes were wide, seeing everything, focusing on nothing.

Princess snorted, tugging softly on the rope.

"Oh!" Rae said. "Sorry." She went along as Princess trotted away from the judge, straight and true, taking the line she always had, going the distance she'd always gone. Then they turned and trotted back to their place in line.

The judge continued onward, considering, marking her card, pausing beside some contestants to jot down their numbers. She handed the ring steward the card with her scores, and he carried it across the ring to the announcer's booth. Princess listened for her own name. It would come first, and there would be a blue ribbon . . .

Not this time. A gleaming quarter horse got the blue and made the victory pass, while Princess left the ring with a white fourth-place ribbon fluttering on her halter. She looked along the rail—she couldn't help it—for a large, proud figure.

Who wasn't there.

~

"*Rae!*" someone said. It was Eden leading Guillaume, both of them as perfectly turned out as if they'd stepped out of a catalog. Rae had seen them in halter class, accepting the red second-place ribbon.

"Hi," she said. Guillaume pricked his ears at the sound of her voice, looking as friendly as she'd ever seen him.

"What a great pony!" Eden said. "Where did you find her?"

"She's . . . not mine." The birthday feeling surged again—the nervous birthday feeling, the what-if-this-isn't-the-year feeling. "I'm riding her at camp."

"*That's* a *camp* pony?"

"She's a Highover pony. One of the rescues."

"I thought those were only old broodmares and the ones he couldn't sell," Eden said. "This pony's *amazing!*" Then she looked at Rae's face. "But that's a problem, right?"

It hadn't been a problem, but suddenly it was. Princess had been amazing in the small, private world of riding camp and in Rae's heart. Today she was amazing out in public, where everyone could see, and she had an owner who wasn't Tish.

"It might—"

The loudspeaker interrupted. "*Contestants, please saddle up for beginner's equitation.*"

"Juniors are after that," Eden said. "We'd better go get ready." She smiled, a little shyly. "It's cool that you're here, Rae."

Dad and Gammer met them at the trailer. Dad introduced himself to Princess, giving her the back of his hand to sniff. Mom had taught him that. "She's beautiful," he said to Rae. "Doesn't look much like Rusty, does she?"

He seemed to want to talk, but Rae didn't have time. She saddled and bridled Princess, taking care not to hurry, to make everything neat and comfortable. When she turned around to get her helmet, he was standing there watching, scratching his chin in that measuring way. A pang of excitement shot through Rae, like a cramp.

Don't think about it. She mounted and rode toward the ring.

"Equitation is all about you," Tish had told them. Riders were judged on how they looked and, more important, how effective they were. Someone riding beautifully on misbehaving pony could, in theory, win. Someone riding beautifully on a very well-behaved pony was more likely to win, though, because the good behavior showed that the riding was correct.

Rae followed Guillaume into the ring, trying to feel the way she'd felt sitting on Rusty, after watching one of Eden's lessons. At the walk she could do it. Then came trot and canter, and things started to come apart. Not all riders seemed to remember what that red ribbon decorating Princess's tail meant. Or maybe they weren't completely in control. Ponies and horses kept coming too close. At first Princess just flattened her ears, but it kept happening, grinding on her nerves until she couldn't help making a dragon face, complete with a breathy gobbling sound that made the judge and steward turn their heads in surprise.

"It's all right," Rae murmured. Then she remembered; she wasn't supposed to talk in the ring.

But she had to keep Princess safe. She stopped thinking about riding well and started thinking about riding fast. That way nobody *could* pass them. They went by rider after rider—including Radish, for once behaving perfectly!—while the announcer said, *"Contestants are reminded that equitation class is not a race!"*

Rae felt herself turn red. She slowed Princess a little, and the hoofbeats behind came closer. Princess flicked back a worried ear. Rae firmed her jaw and sped up again. It was no surprise at all that equitation ended with her not getting a ribbon, and with the judge beckoning. Rae rode over to her, turning red again. This would be a lecture. She had disgraced Tish's teaching—

"Good job taking care of your pony," the judge said. "I could see she was getting anxious, and I liked that you kept her out of trouble. She may settle down as the day goes on. Keep trying!"

"That's almost better than a ribbon," Tish said, when Rae told her about it.

There was time to go back to the trailer and give Princess a drink during the senior and Western equitation classes. That was when Sam and Tully arrived. "Mom brought us so we could cheer for you," Sam said.

"Our camps finished yesterday," Tully said. "So—this is your camp pony? What's his name?"

"Her name. Princess."

"Is she as wonderful as she looks?"

Rae couldn't even get close to saying yes.

"Uh-oh," Sam said. She and Tully exchanged a twin look. "You weren't going to fall in love for real. There was this whole plan."

"Well how could she not," Tully said. "Even I can see—but you're okay, right?"

"How can she be okay?" Sam asked.

"But you are, aren't you?" Tully said. "You look happy."

"She looks exhausted," Sam said.

"*And* happy. And—scared? Why?"

"Because—" No, Rae couldn't say it, not even to them. Because what was there to say? Dad scratching his chin, pacing off the paddock space, a random word here and there from Gammer—it all added up to something big to her, but Tully's scientific mind might see through it, Sam's storytelling mind might find a flaw in the logic. "I have to get ready for pleasure class," she said.

Pleasure class was about calm good manners, a pleasant appearance, energy that was perfectly under control. It wasn't about speed and dragon faces. "Ribbons don't matter," Rae told Sam and Tully afterward. "Besides, in real life Princess is *total* pleasure!"

Their last class before lunch was junior trail. That started with all contestants gathering in the ring to walk, trot, and canter. Ponies were getting a little tired by now, the ring was more orderly, and suddenly Princess was herself. Rae could feel it in her straight-arrow trot, and her lifting, merry-go-round canter, see it in her pricked ears. "*Perfect!*" she whispered, and one silvery ear pointed back at her for a moment, listening. Tears prickled Rae's eyes. *Please*, she thought—only thought it, but the ear tipped back again.

When they'd gone both ways, lined up in the center, and each backed a few steps under the judge's eyes, they left the ring and waited while volunteers set up an obstacle course. Then, one at a time, each contestant rode across a little bridge, backed through an L made of poles, dropped a loop of rope over the horns of a plywood cow, and hopped over a small jump.

Princess watched. This was not something she'd ever done at a show. It resembled the games they'd played at camp. Rae *cared* about those games.

All right, then! Princess entered the ring proudly, almost prancing. Rae, who'd started off feeling all the eyes on her, came back to herself. *We're supposed to walk*, she said, with a light touch on the reins, a deeper seat in the saddle. Princess slowed and lowered her head. Her hooves rattled across the bridge. Smoothly and accurately, she backed between the poles, never touching one. She approached the plywood cow without hesitation and stood like a rock while Rae roped it.

Now came the jump, a simple low pole between two wings made of brush. Princess trotted up to it at the measured, sober speed Rae asked for. But measured and sober weren't how she felt right now. This was a *jump*. Rae was on her back. She bounded high over the pole with a sassy flick of her hind feet at the top of the arc. Cheers went up from the grandstand. Rae could hear Sam and Tully chanting, "Prin-*cess!* Prin-*cess!*"

This time they did win a ribbon, a lovely yellow silk rosette for third place. "I could *swear* I know this pony," the judge murmured as she pinned it on. The ribbon fluttered on Princess's bridle as they left the ring. Princess tipped her ears toward the rail and her nostrils flared, but she didn't catch the scent she was searching for.

a thin old man

Now it was time for lunch. The trees at the edge of the field cast a welcome shade in which to spread blankets and unpack picnic baskets. This was the end-of-camp celebration, so parents and other family joined them; Rae included Sam and Tully as honorary family members. Tish shared slices of Gammer's strawberry-rhubarb pie and made a speech mentioning each person's accomplishments. Steve had learned the trick of keeping Nubbin moving. Amber had not fallen off Radish once. And Rae? "Rae learned every single thing I tried to teach her," Tish said. "Or else she was born knowing."

Rae turned red and looked away. Down by the ring she noticed the judge talking to a white-haired lady in a hot-pink sun visor. They both looked up the hill. At Princess?

Yes, definitely at Princess.

Sam and Tully turned to see what Rae was watching. After a minute, the old lady took out her phone and held it up.

"She's taking a picture," Tully said.

"Now she's sending it to someone," Sam said, as the pink visor tilted down and the lady's thumbs started to move. "Is that okay? People aren't supposed to take pictures of kids without permission."

"Ponies are different," Rae said. "I think." But she felt uneasy. She went over and untied Princess, and brought her to graze near them while they finished lunch.

The loudspeaker came on soon afterward. *"We'll be starting the afternoon classes in twenty minutes. First up is costume class, then children's leadline, and then we'll ask our volunteers to set up the course for junior jumping."*

"Rae, come help!" Steve called.

"Everybody come help!" Amber said. Spare hands were needed to hold things, tape things, wire things. Rae was good at remembering how the costumes were supposed to go together. Dad was good at making them actually work, because of all the things he carried in his pockets: a multitool, paper clips, bread twist ties, string.

Barely in time, the costumes were assembled, and everyone streamed toward the ring. This was the beginning of the afternoon fun, with games and races instead of formal classes. More people were arriving by the minute.

In the ring Rae spotted Eden leading Guillaume, who carried a small glittery model of the Eiffel Tower on his saddle. Eden's tall leather boots were fastened into the stirrups, with a long loaf of French bread poking out the top of each, and he had a French flag draped across his haunches. Hardly anyone knew there was such a thing as a French Saddle Pony so nobody understood the costume, but it got a lot of cheers. Everyone got a lot of cheers.

Ribbons were distributed, many more than in a normal class. Then came leadline, the slowest halter class of all. Tiny children, some with a spotter on each side, were led at a snail's pace around the ring, beaming, waving to their fans, making loud and funny comments. Every child got a ribbon, the cheering was thunderous, and then—

"First call for the junior jumping class. Riders, make your way toward the ring, please."

Rae felt a shudder of show nerves. They were new jumpers, she and Princess. They didn't know much, and everyone would be watching. A lot more everyones than earlier in the day—*don't think about that.* She brushed Princess and spritzed her with fly spray, tacked up, buckled on her helmet, and rode toward the gate, where the junior riders were gathering. Last class . . . ever? Or—*don't think.* She should watch her friends and cheer, as they would cheer her.

Radish had behaved well all morning. He was done with that. He raced around the course, missed several fences altogether, took one down, and skidded to a stop at the last one. Amber slid off over his neck, landed neatly on her feet on the other side, and raised both hands in the air in a victory sign.

Nubbin walked to the first fence and stood blinking at it. Steve laughed till he got hiccups.

Banner, the tallest of Tish's horses, was a dashing jumper,

but seldom remembered to pick up his feet. Poles scattered everywhere. Volunteers followed him around, putting them back up.

Riders from Briarwood did much better, and Eden and Guillaume had a near-perfect round. Only at the last jump, a car door slamming distracted Guillaume, and he touched a rail, which trembled and tottered. Rae held her breath—they all did—until the rail wobbled back into place on its peg. The crowd cheered.

Meanwhile, out in the section of field marked off for handicapped parking, a wispy lady went around to the back of her station wagon and took out a wheelchair. She helped a thin, trembling old man settle into it, then started pushing him over the bumpy ground. He sat bolt upright, pointing toward the ring with his whole arm.

They were almost there when the announcer said, *"The next contestant will be Rae Mitchell, riding Princess."* The old man clutched the arms of his chair, rocking in frustration. With flutters and apologies, the lady got people to make space for them at the rail as Rae and Princess entered the ring.

Rae snuck one quick glance at the grandstand. *So* many people. She forced herself to look straight in front of her. Princess pricked her ears toward the jumps. At Rae's signal, she swished her tail and picked up her slow, merry-go-round canter.

Eden, or any Briarwood rider, would have brought her to the first fence more slowly and chosen the perfect spot for takeoff. Rae just gave Princess her head. They thundered to the jump and Princess soared over, landing lightly as a bird. Rae pointed her toward the next. That was all the help she could give—remembering the course, telling Princess where to go, staying out of her way. They came at the fences fast and cleared each one with an extravagant bound while the crowd went wild with cheering. Rae barely heard them. She was in a tunnel, a beautiful tunnel, with only one thing to do: rise in the saddle, fold at the hips, float her hands forward along Princess's reaching neck, and ride out the leap, then soften into the landing and turn her head to look toward the next jump.

Which, suddenly, was the last jump. A lump in her throat swelled and hurt, yet couldn't cancel the sweetness. "*I love you, Princess!*" she whispered. They rose, they soared, and in midair Princess's head snapped around, as she smelled something familiar.

Near the ring fence.

A scent she'd been missing for a long, long time.

She changed angle in midair, landed roughly, stopped. A rail thudded to the ground behind her. She flicked one ear back at it, then stared at the suddenly silent crowd along the ring fence—

There!

A thin old man wrapped in a blanket sat in a wheelchair, gazing between the rails with enormous eyes. A scent drifted from him, medicine-tinged, yet sweet, beloved . . .

Could it be? The shape was different, the scent had changed. Still, couldn't it be him?

It could. It was.

A loud whinny burst from Princess's throat. She lifted into her lovely, reaching, Connemara trot, tail high, neck arched, and carried Rae straight to him.

chapter 38

partners

At the fence Princess thrust her head between the rails, nickering softly. Roland brought his thin hands up to her face and opened his mouth. No words came out, just a sound. *"Pnss. Mmm Prinssss."*

He was smaller now. His shaky hands were empty and his voice a husky, broken whisper. None of that mattered. Princess breathed him in deep, while his tears trickled onto her mane and ears. Everything inside her felt warm and sweet.

Rae sat on her back, frozen.

How did they get out of the ring? Was it Tish who led Princess, or Dad? However it happened, whoever did it, after a bit she was outside the ring, still on Princess's back, with everyone gathered around—Dad and Gammer, Sam and Tully. Eden even. Tish was there, giving Rae's knee a squeeze as she said to the woman behind the wheelchair, "We haven't met, but I think I know you. I'm Tish."

The woman sniffed and dabbed at her eyes. "I'm Cecile

Calloway. We've talked on the phone about this pony often, but I never dreamed she was so important to Uncle. He tried to ask me about her weeks ago, and I didn't understand. Then Mrs. Portchester called me an hour ago, and—"

Now Mrs. Portchester was there too, beaming under her pink visor. "It's her, isn't it, Roland! Your Princess. Though how she got here I've no idea."

"She was very ill," Tish said. "I took her home with me the day they were discovered, to make sure she got special care. Cecile and I have been in touch—"

"Yet neither of you knew who she was?" Mrs. Portchester asked. "I suppose you wouldn't, though, and Roland couldn't tell anyone to look for her. She was his pride and joy, you know. He used to say, 'I wouldn't take a million dollars for her.'"

A dull, prickling chill spread through Rae. *That* pony. She'd fallen in love with *that* pony. She wanted to slide out of the saddle and disappear into the crowd, but she couldn't move.

"Well!" Mrs. Portchester said. "I've got to keep this show moving." She bustled away, and in a moment her voice came out of the loudspeaker. "*Sorry for the delay. Here are the winners of the junior jumping class.*"

The winner was Eden. Sitting up there on Princess, Rae could see as clearly as in a dream: the judge pinning the blue ribbon on Guillaume's bridle, him cantering around the ring in all his dark beauty as the crowd cheered.

When he and Eden had come out the gate Mrs. Portchester said, "*In second place we have a pony known to you for most of the day as 'Princess.' In fact, she's a champion Connemara whose real name is Highover Bonphrionsa. She's owned by my dear friend*

Roland McDermott, and the two of them have just been reunited!
She was one of the ponies abandoned at Highover, she spent most
of this summer as a camp pony—and the young woman who's
ridden her so well all day is Miss Rae Mitchell."

The sound of her name woke Rae from her trance. She looked up and Gammer was there, closer than she'd realized. Their eyes met.

"Spine of steel, lovebug," Gammer said quietly.

Spine of steel. Rae straightened in the saddle and shortened her reins. Would Princess respond? Would she let Rae ride her away from this old man she loved?

She didn't want to. Rae could feel that. Reluctance made her steps short and tense, and she kept looking back at him. But after a moment her ears relaxed, and her whole body softened. Rae felt that, too—the decision to trust. This was *Rae*.

"That's right," Rae said, her voice choking. "I'll take you right back to him."

The ribbon presentation was a blur. The judge looking compassionate: "You've had quite a day!" The brilliant red ribbon against Princess's silver neck. A lot of noise, a lot of faces. Then they were back outside the ring, part of the group around the wheelchair, with Princess resting her chin on the old man's shoulder.

Behind them horses and riders were gathering for the next class, and the area near the gate was crowded. "These people have a horse show to run," Tish said. "Let's go up to my trailer where it's shady, and have a talk. I don't have anyone in the next couple of classes, so we have a little time."

Dad pushed the wheelchair up the hill. Princess followed

it. She felt different to Rae. Tired, probably, but also deeply relaxed. Some tension that had always been there was gone.

A crowd followed behind them: Tish and Ms. Calloway, of course, Dad and Gammer, Sam and Tully, a random smattering of campers. Kayla, Eden's instructor, joined them for some reason, and Eden on Guillaume brought up the rear.

As they neared the trailer Princess veered off toward her own water pail, left warming in the sun. Rae slid down and let her have a few thirsty gulps. Then she took off the saddle and bridle, slipped on the halter, and sponged Princess's sweaty back and the hot, damp places behind her ears. The old man sat leaning forward in his wheelchair, watching all this hungrily.

Now her face. Princess leaned into the cool wetness, closing her eyes. Rae was here. *He* was here. It was a joy that almost hurt. She would like to graze now, perhaps a little distance from them, and bite by sweet bite find her way to calm.

But people needed to *talk* their way to calm. They gathered in the deepest, coolest part of the shade, Tish on a mounting block, the old man in his chair, everyone else circling around. The grass here was wispy and weedy. Princess nipped at it, while Rae stood leaning back against her side. That felt good to both of them, steadying.

"So," Tish said. "The question of Princess." Rae saw that Roland McDermott thought there was no *question* of Princess. Her stomach twisted.

"I'm happy to take her home with me today," Tish said, "and keep her as long as she needs a place to stay. Or I could trailer her to Highover—"

A terrible blankness came over the old man's face. Ms.

Calloway shook her head. "Uncle lives in town now. I think he'll always have to."

"Maybe you're interested in selling her, then?" Eden's instructor Kayla pushed forward. "That pony is a natural jumper. I could certainly find a place for her at Briarwood."

Roland McDermott's face lit up. He opened his mouth. No sound came out, but he shook his head decisively, mouthing words he couldn't manage to say. Rae knew what they were.

Kayla hadn't become successful in the horse world by taking no for an answer. "She's too good a pony to just sit idle. At my stable I could match her with the right rider—"

"She *has* the right rider!" Eden said. "*Rae!*"

"Exactly," Tish said. "When Princess came to me, she was frozen inside, and no wonder, after what she'd been through. Being a lesson pony didn't suit her at all. But she blossomed once Rae started riding her—and not just riding her. *Loving* her. Doting on her." She turned to Dad and Gammer. "Before I knew who she was, I'd been planning to ask if you could give Princess a home. Would you have considered it?"

The question. It had never occurred to Rae that somebody else might ask it.

"We were working ourselves up to ask *you*," Dad said. "If you thought there was enough pasture."

"Princess can't have much grass," Tish said. "She's been starved, so her body responds differently. She may always need to be on a diet."

"But I gather she's very valuable," Dad said glumly. "And she belongs to this gentleman."

All eyes turned to Roland McDermott. He sat slumped in

his chair, looking fragile, yet powerfully stubborn, the way Rae had seen him sitting in front of Princess's stall door that day at Highover. *I wouldn't take a million dollars for her.* That wasn't Princess's real price, she knew. It was his way of saying, *There is no price.* He didn't know what he would or could do, but he would never give her up, as long as he had breath in his body.

Could Rae blame him? She would feel exactly the same.

"Well I don't see the problem," Sam said, breaking the awkward silence. "*You*, sir, can't take care of her."

"And *you* can't afford her," Tully told Rae.

"So it's easy!" Sam said. "Be partners! Mr.—whatever your name is—you can buy the hay—"

"—and Rae will do the work," Tully said. "No one could do it better!"

"Exactly!" Tish said. "If you want someone to show Princess, that's Rae. If you want someone to love her and make her happy, that's Rae too. As I'm sure you can see."

At these words the old man looked hard at Rae. Rae looked back at him, though it was difficult. He wasn't an easy person to face in all his shattered power. She made herself do it, though, with Princess warm and damp at her back.

At last he stirred, turning from one person to the next, searching faces deeply, coming finally back to Rae.

"*Trssst?*" he asked.

"Trust?" Gammer asked. "You can trust Rae. With Princess? You can trust Rae to the moon and back."

Tish said, "Rae has educated herself more thoroughly and worked harder than any child I've ever known."

"And she's Rae." A few people seemed to be saying that—Dad, Tish, Eden. Rae's heart swelled.

But the old man needed something more. He needed to be asked. Could she do that? For years she'd taught herself not to ask. That was the way she stayed strong, took care of Dad, took care of herself.

Spine of steel, she thought. Right now it felt like a spine of pudding. She took a deep, gulping breath. "Could I take care of her for you?" It was hard to speak past the hot cherry-pit lump in her throat. "I—I love her too."

He lifted his head and looked straight at her, for what seemed like a long time. Then he reached out his hand.

You ask, you get an answer. Rae gave him the lead rope.

Or would have, but Princess saw the hand too. She stretched her silver muzzle toward it, shifting her weight, tilting Rae in his direction. He shook his head, tears spilling down his cheeks, and held up two fingers, close together. "*Ppprt—*"

"Partners, Uncle?" Ms. Calloway asked. He closed his eyes in agreement and opened them. Yes, that was what he meant.

Rae took the outstretched hand. It was soft and trembling. She was stronger than he was, though he was so old and rich and proud.

She didn't have any more words left to say. She nodded, and he nodded, and Princess nudged both hands lightly, blowing her soft breath over them.

epilogue

The handshake decided everything, but much still had to happen before Princess could come to her new home: a legal agreement for one, and lawyers don't work quickly. But the outlines of one were soon drawn up. Princess would belong to both Rae and Roland. She could never be sold without both agreeing, and all decisions about her care must be unanimous.

That looked like a stretch at first. Roland had notions about how his Princess should be housed, which were hard to fit into the reality of the old barn, yet hard to say no to when he was paying. Tish was helpful there, able to interpret and negotiate. In the end Dad built a simple, roomy box stall next to his shop, with a half door that looked directly out into the yard. Rae could see it from her bedroom window.

Dad put up a fence around the plot of grass in the backyard and made a smaller paddock for Princess to stay in when she wasn't grazing. A load of sweet-smelling hay arrived from Roland's hay supplier. Princess's monogrammed blankets, feed and water tubs, and personal grooming kit were delivered from Highover, along with a handsome tack trunk to put them all in.

While all this was happening, and Rae was visiting Princess at Tish's as often as Gammer's pie route took her in that direction, news broke that Charlie and Darlene Baker had been arrested. An antique bowl stolen from Highover Farm had been traced to Darlene. When Charlie learned what had happened to the field ponies, he agreed to testify against her. "I'm not an honest man," he said in his statement, "but I draw the line at cruelty." His wife pled not guilty and was jailed pending trial, as she was considered to be a flight risk.

What Roland McDermott thought about all this was impossible to know. Rae could read his feelings very well. His eyes flashed anger, sank in shame, stared into the distance puzzled and confused, but he could put none of this into words yet. All he could do is look fiercely at Rae and repeat, "*Trrrst!*"

She didn't know what to say to that at first, but the best answer, the one that made him smile, was "*Partners.*"

When the stall and paddock were final, Cecile Calloway drove her uncle and Rae over to Tish's. Rae thought it was important for them to be there when Princess was put onto the trailer. "We can't explain what's happening," she said, "but at least she'll know it's us."

When they walked into the barn, Princess let out a whinny. It had been a confusing, anxious couple of weeks without seeing Rae every day, or him. But they were here now. That was what mattered.

Rae put on the resplendent monogrammed blanket. Tish showed her how to fasten the shipping bandages around Princess's legs.

"Your Majesty!" Tish said, bowing. Princess didn't understand, but there was a light-hearted, excited feeling in the air as Tish led her onto the trailer.

Meanwhile, another reunion was taking place. The cat had watched Roland for several minutes, tested his scent on the air, considered. Finally he lofted into Roland's lap, thinner and bonier than it used to be. Roland gave him a chin scratch that was as good as ever.

"You must know this cat," Tish said. "He came with Princess." Roland nodded. The cat purred.

"He's a barn cat here," Tish said. "But it looks like he might be willing to transition to a lap cat. Can you have pets where you live?"

He could, and by the reluctance the cat showed to get down when it was time to leave, it appeared that he soon would.

"Ride with me?" Tish asked. Rae nodded. She would have ridden in the trailer with Princess, if Tish would've allowed it.

"I'll miss Princess," Tish said, as she drove out of the yard. "Maybe you'll bring her back to camp next year, Rae. I do sometimes have campers who bring their own ponies. Or you and Roland might decide to take her to Briarwood."

"I'd rather come here," Rae said. But it would be fun to ride with Eden sometimes.

Was this real, though? These plans, these decisions? It hardly seemed possible. She had to keep looking back at the trailer, which had Princess in it, and at the station wagon following them, which contained the old man. She could foresee that it would sometimes be complicated, but just now she was so happy it hurt.

Here was her house, finally with Gammer's apartment parked beside the blueberry bushes and a welcome party waiting, complete with a banner, Sam and Tully, Eden, two dogs and three pies.

Tish parked and then backed Princess down the ramp. She handed the lead rope to Rae. "She's all yours—and yours," she added, as Roland's eyes flashed.

Princess tested the air. She smelled grass and ripe fruit. Chickens—that was a new thing. No ponies. It seemed a noisy place, with dogs barking and girls squealing. But those were all familiar sounds and beneath them was a sense of peace.

She went with Rae, out behind the house, where there was a pony after all, galloping straight toward her. Princess flattened her ears, warning him to keep his distance.

But he wasn't actually moving. Rae led her closer. Princess sniffed cautiously and found that he was a thing, pony shaped—so that was okay, and the grass tasted delicious.

Rae led her to a stall and small paddock, took off the bandages and blanket, and unsnapped the rope. Exploring, Princess found a salt lick, her own buckets, a net full of familiar-tasting hay. And Rae was here. The whole place smelled of her. Princess settled down to eat.

Gammer served pie—raspberry, the first of the season. "I think raspberry is his favorite," Rae told Gammer, when Roland nearly burst into tears at his first bite.

"Wait till you taste my peach pie, sir, before you make up

your mind," Gammer said. "In fact, wait a whole year. You have no idea what all's in store for you!"

He was reluctant to go home, but at last it was time. He was working the wheelchair himself by now, and motored over to Princess's fence alone, and sat talking with her. Rae would have liked to know what he was saying, but she didn't follow. That was between them.

He and Eden left early, and a little later Sam and Tully's mother came to pick them up. Rae walked out to the car with them.

"So," Tully said. "You have a pony."

"*The* pony," Sam said. "Just the kind of story ending I like."

Rae waved goodbye and went indoors to help Gammer wash up the dishes. "Didn't I tell you, lovebug?" Gammer said, handing her a pie plate to dry. "Here we are looking out at your pony, right there in the backyard."

"Is it okay to be this happy?" Rae asked. Her chest ached with joy, her eyes felt dry and tired with it.

"Perfectly okay," Gammer said. "Don't let anyone tell you otherwise. And if happiness turns out to have a few details we didn't expect—that's just the spice in the pie, my love."

"This is a very good pie, Gammer."

⁓

Princess spent the afternoon grazing the new grass, watching the dogs play, listening to the voices. This place had a settled feel to it, a home feeling.

Supper came, the same supper as at Tish's, and darkness fell. That evening, under a bright full moon, it was Rae who came to Princess's stall to do the last check. Rae who lingered at the half door, while Princess breathed against her cheek. Rae who remembered, after a few minutes, to reach into her pocket and pull something out.

"He left a box of these for you."

Princess fumbled it off Rae's open palm—a lump of delicious brown sugar. It said everything that needed to be said, in a perfectly understandable language.

Love love love.